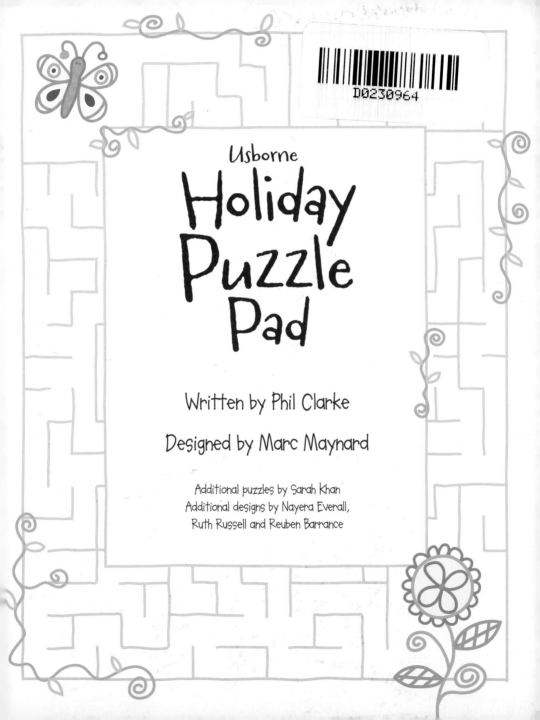

Usborne

Holiday Puzzle Pad

Written by Phil Clarke

Designed by Marc Maynard

Additional puzzles by Sarah Khan
Additional designs by Nayera Everall,
Ruth Russell and Reuben Barrance

1

Pencil pick-up

Write down the order in which you can pick up these pencils, one by one, without disturbing those underneath.

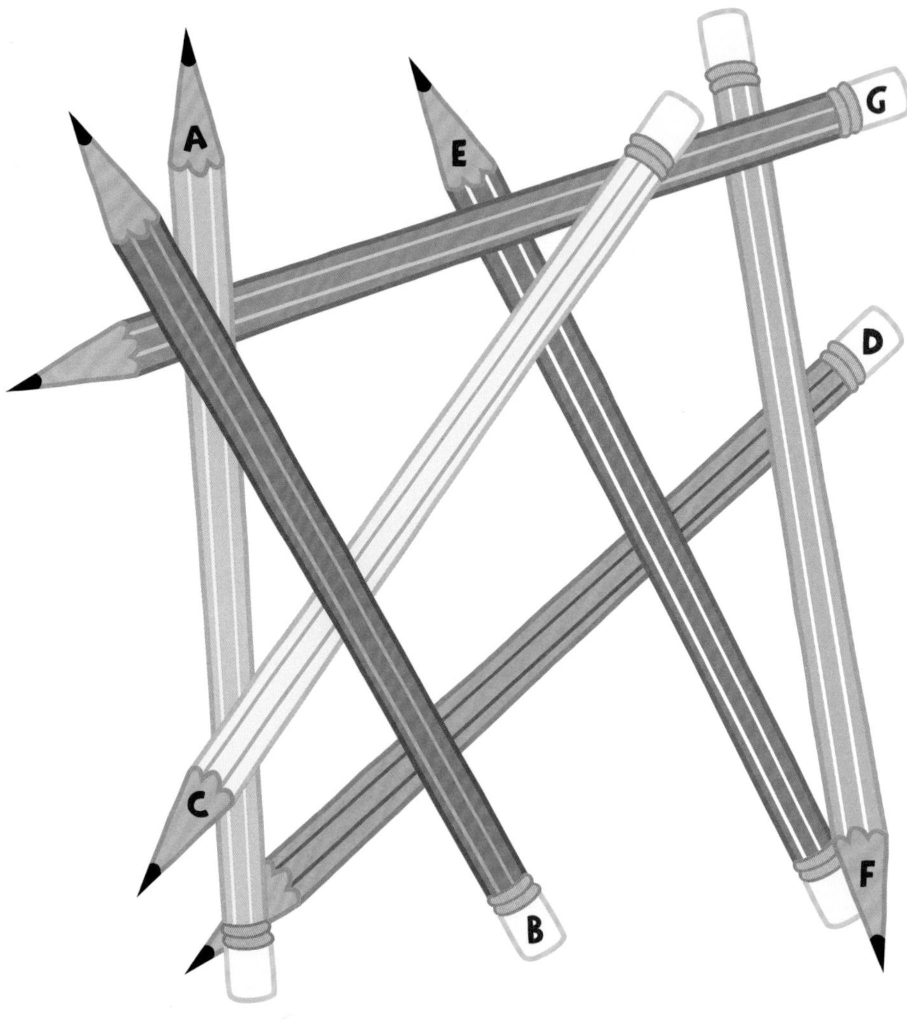

Answer: ....

2 Honeycomb hexagons

Fit the words into the honeycomb. Each word starts in a bright yellow cell and winds clockwise around an orange cell.

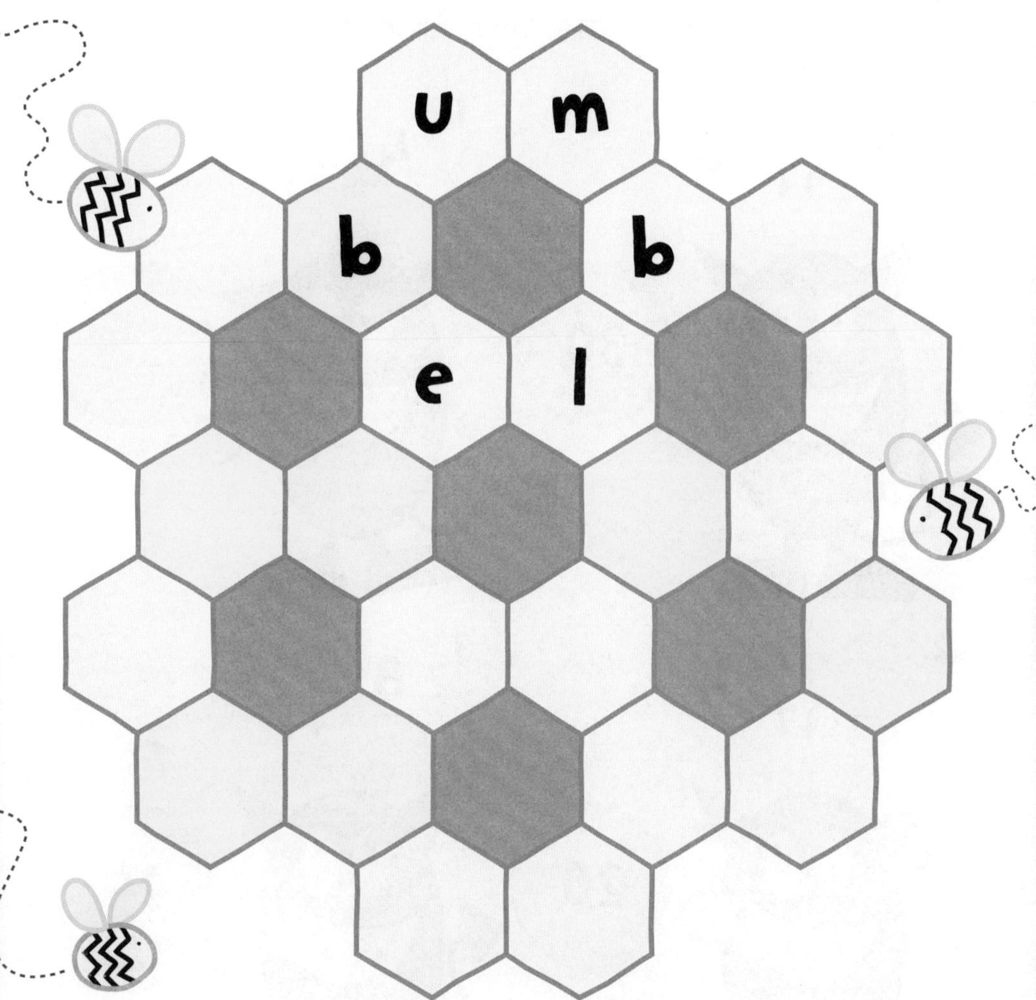

delete detail rubbed elbows

plates ~~bumble~~ worded

Number monster

This little monster eats numbers, chews them up, then spits out new numbers. Find out what the monster does to all the numbers it eats, then fill in the gaps below.

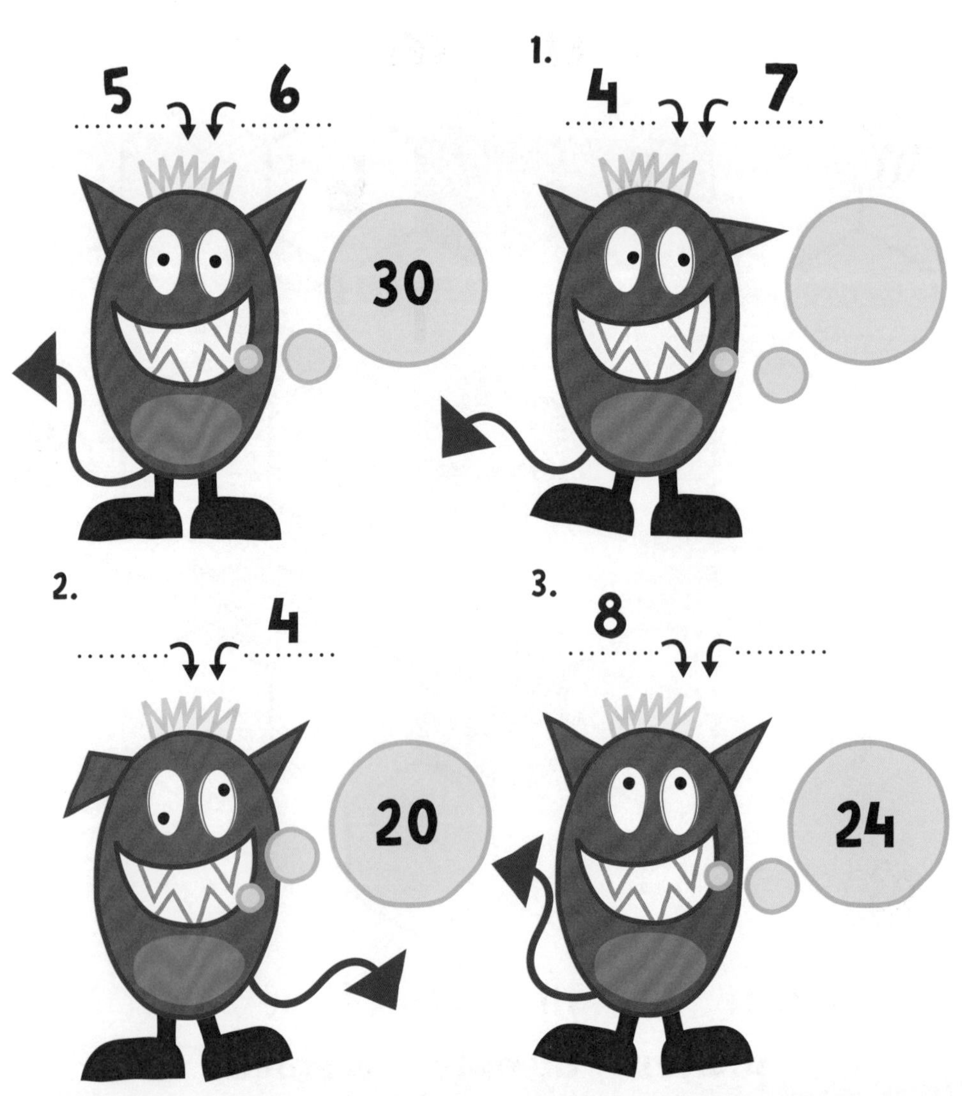

4

Patchwork puzzle

Draw around the two blocks of squares in the patchwork pattern that match the pieces shown below.

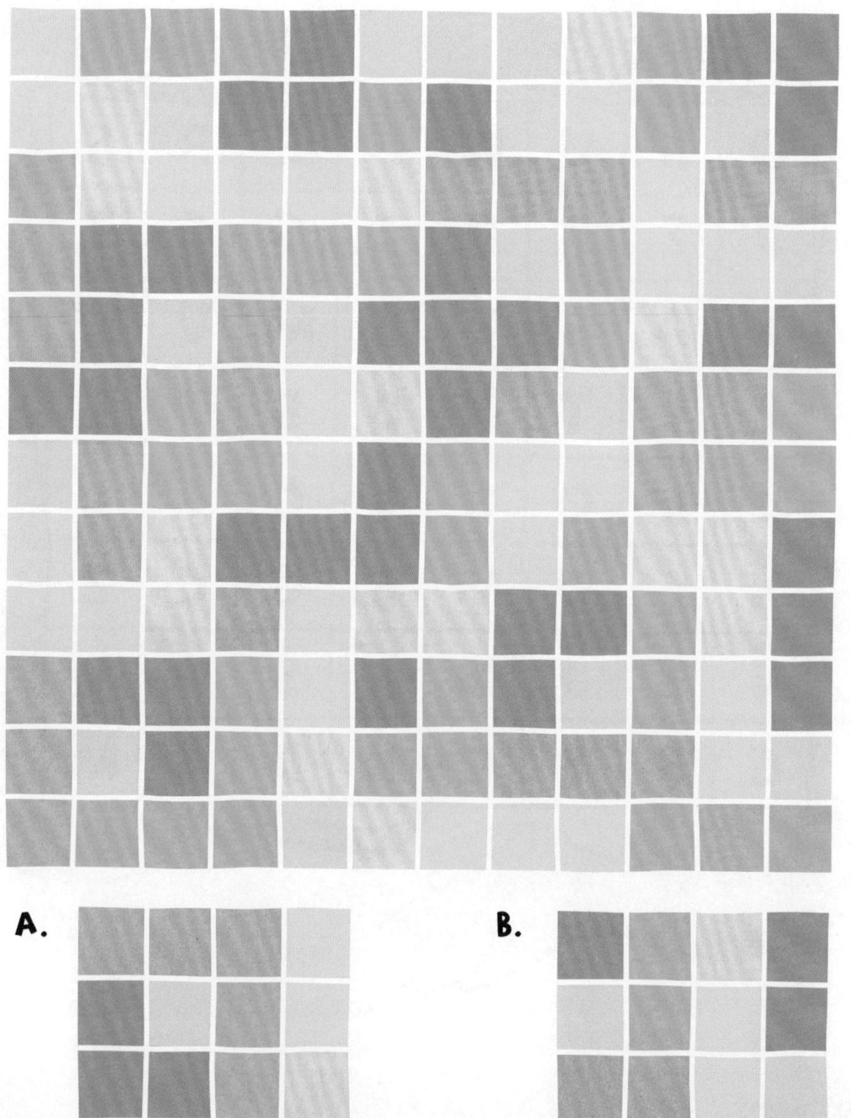

5

Hiss!

Cross out all the letters in the grid that appear more than once to reveal a snake with a powerful grip.

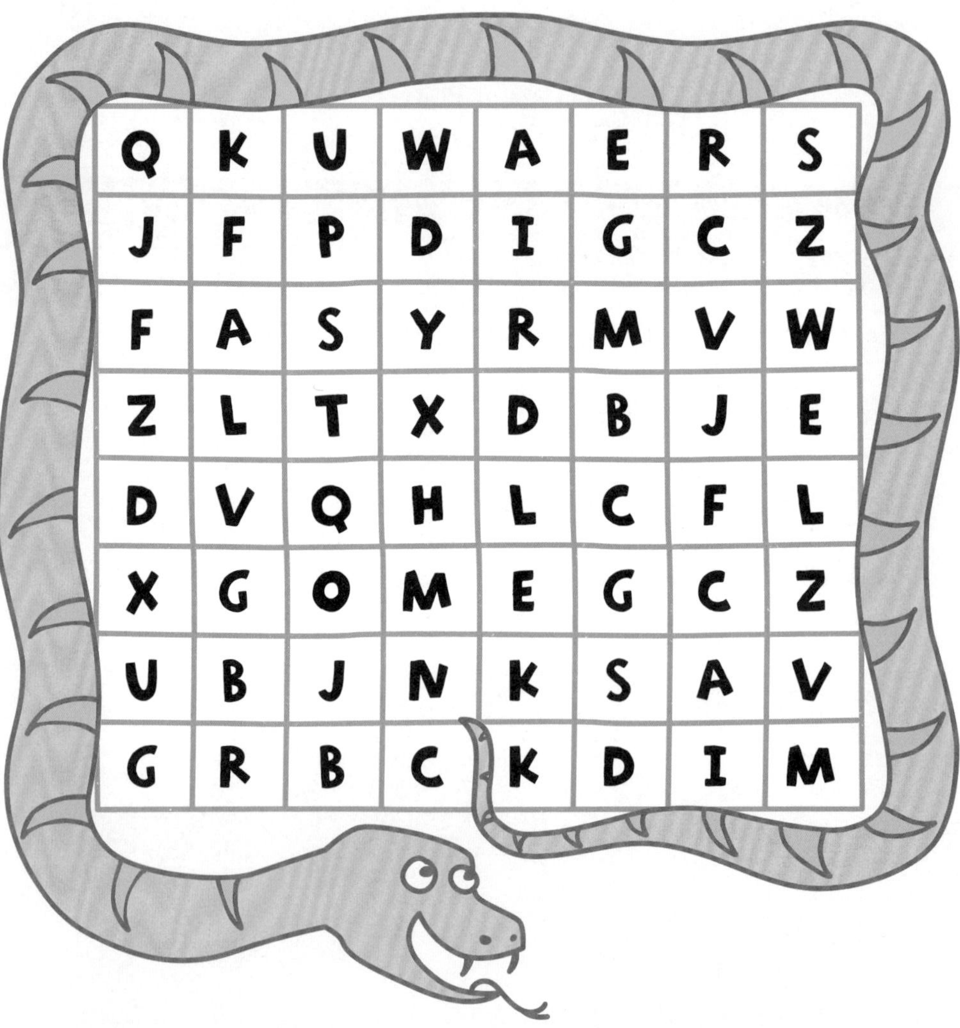

Answer: ....

6

Baggage tags

These suitcases have lost their baggage tags. Use the clues below to find out whose bag is whose, then draw lines to connect each suitcase to its owner's name.

Fay and Gino each have a red suitcase.

Chris, Suki and Fay's suitcases are covered with labels.

Billie and Ravi have small suitcases.

Suki and Billie have green suitcases.

Who?

Join up the dots to see who is sitting in the tree.

Double vision

Copy the drawings across into the blank spaces to see two complete pictures of a knight.

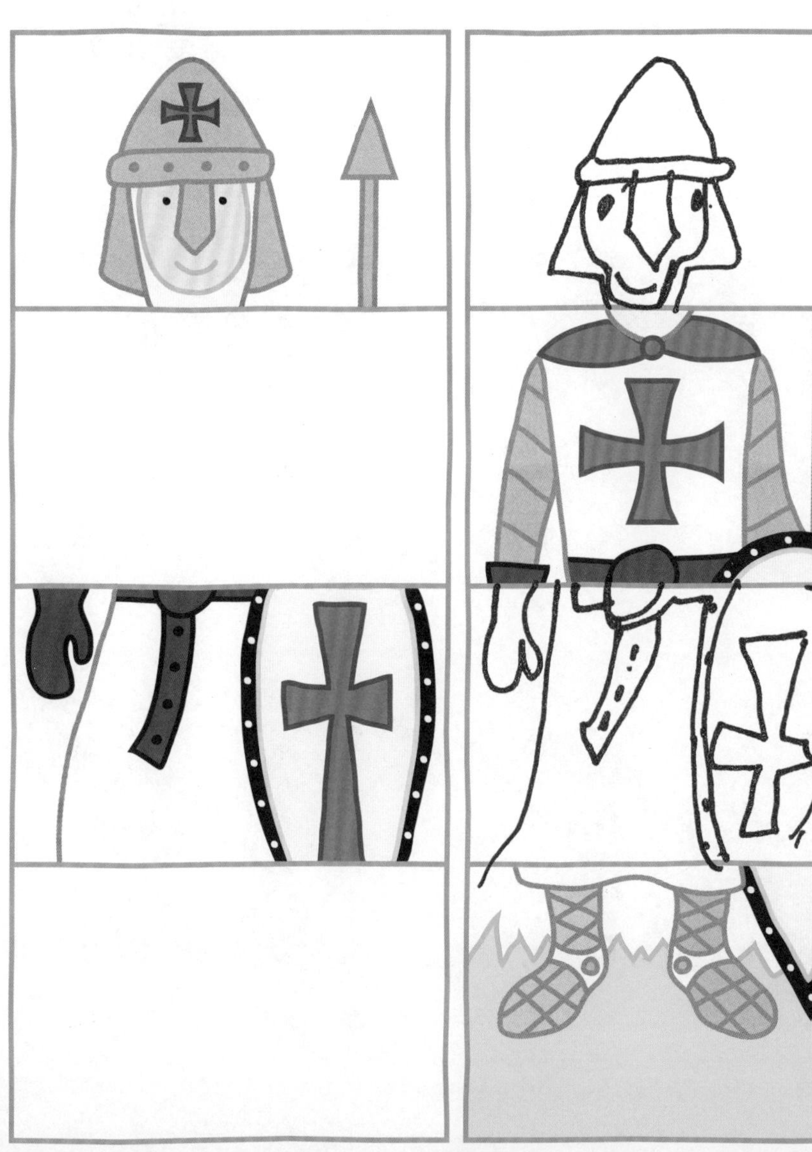

9

Word cross

Put a letter in the middle of each cross to make three-letter words in its arms.

1. G A I P O I T E

2. T E G O E I S R

3. O W A Y L E A T

4. F A A W U I O M

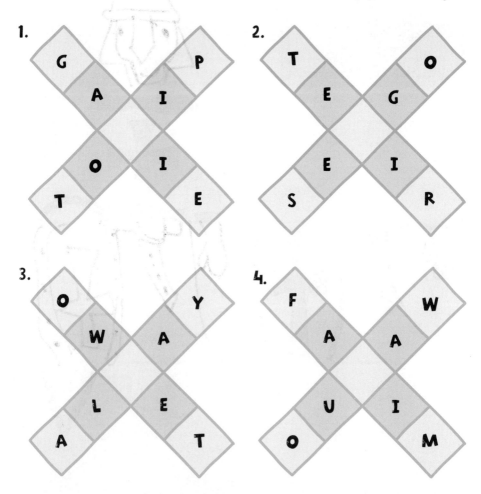

Odd one out

Draw a circle around the odd one out.

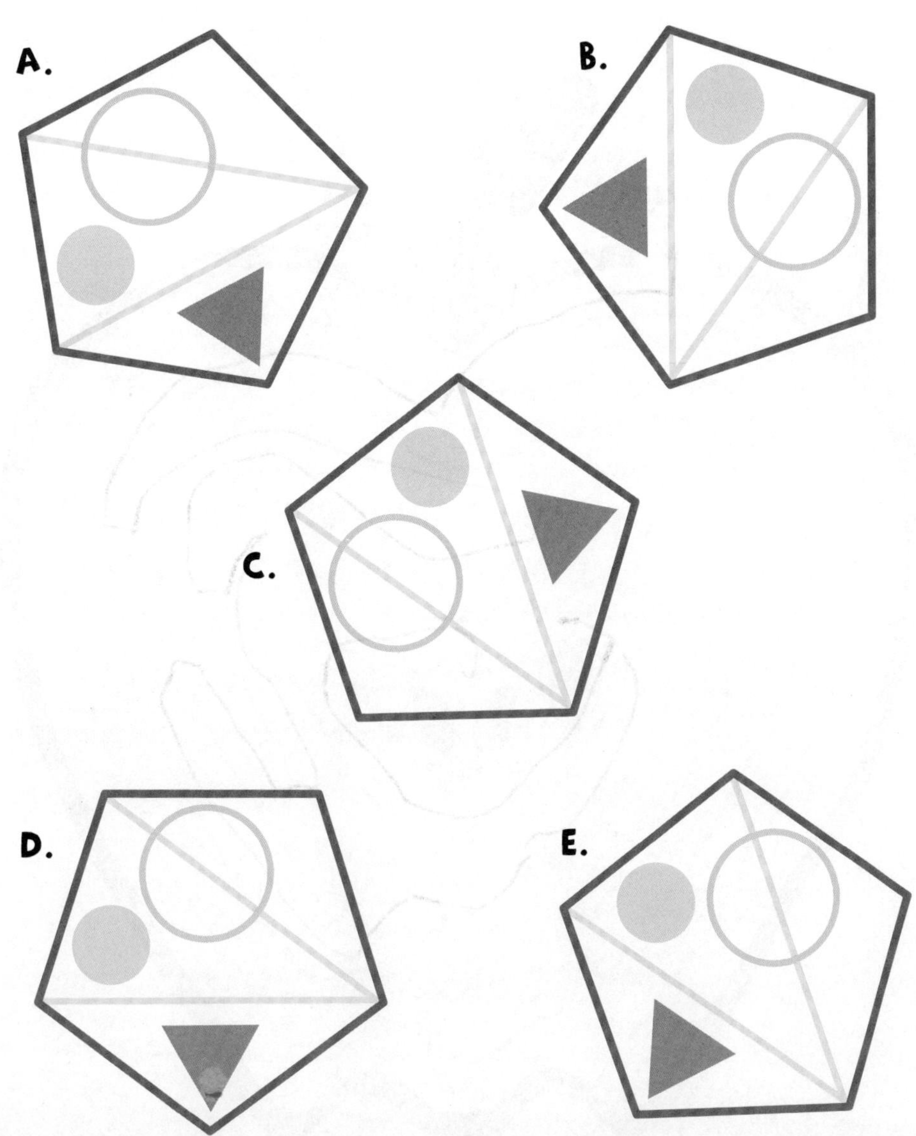

Apple maze

Help the worm wiggle its way to the middle of the apple.

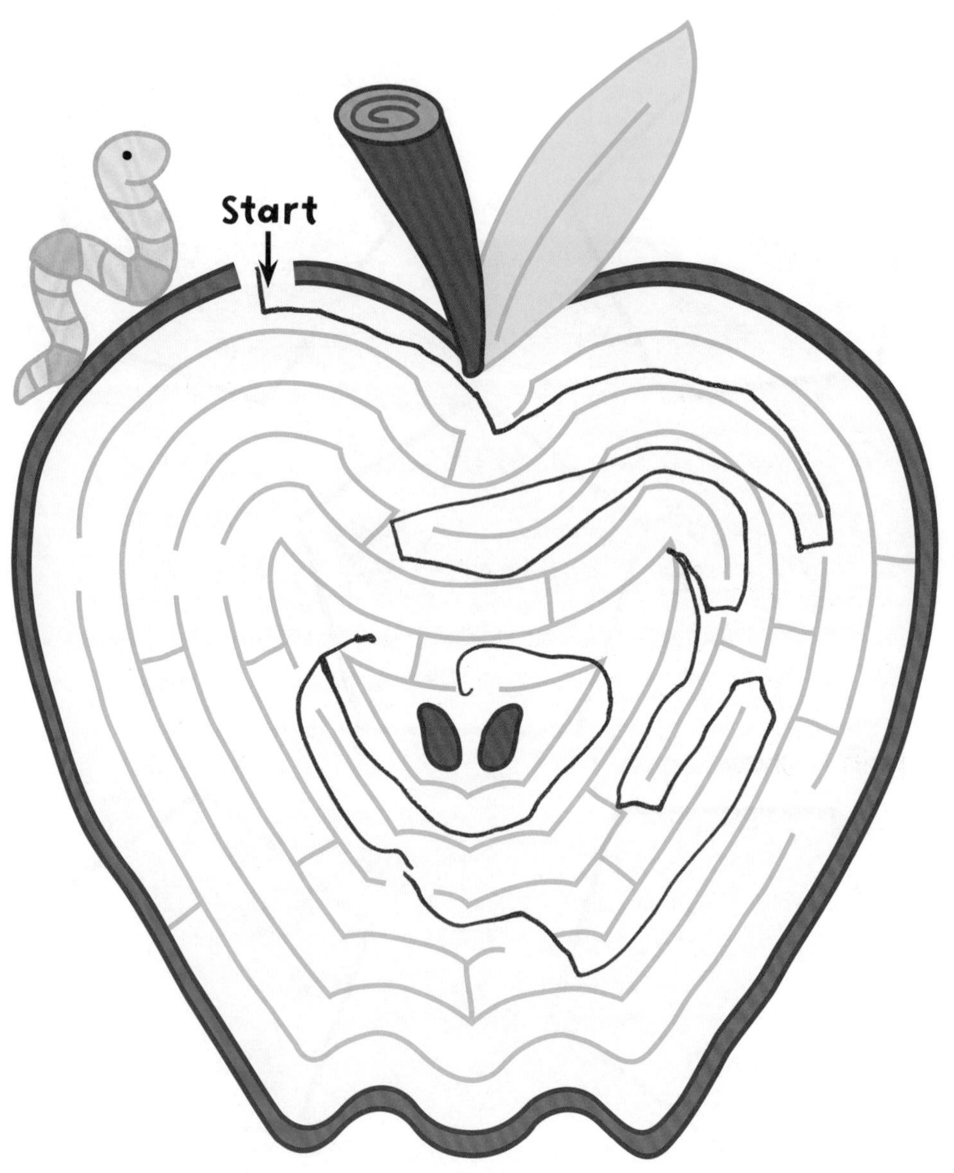

Spot the spots

How many bright red spots are there on this page?

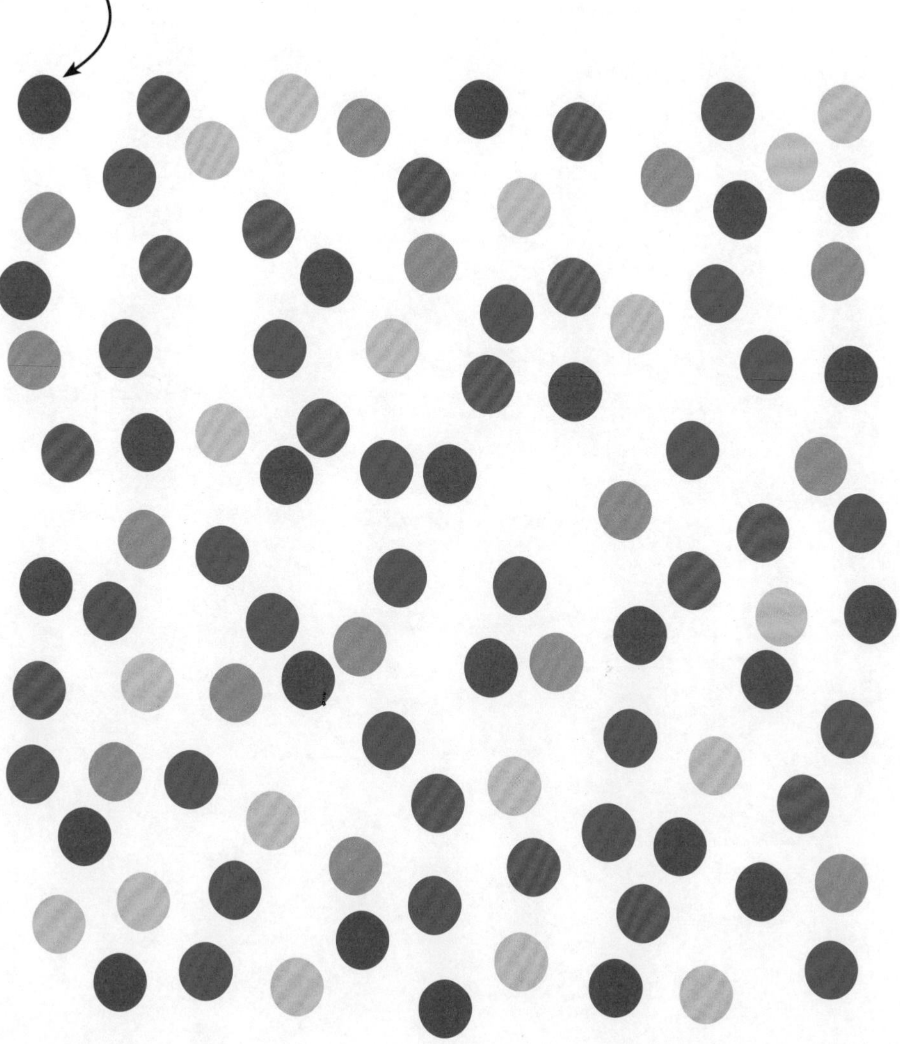

Answer:..

Celebration

Find out which eight letters of the alphabet are missing from this page, then unscramble them to find out why Harry is celebrating.

Square numbers

Use these clues to find the missing numbers and write them on the squares:

- Each number in a red square is 4 more than the number in the orange square next to it.
- Each number in a green square is double the number in the red square next to it.

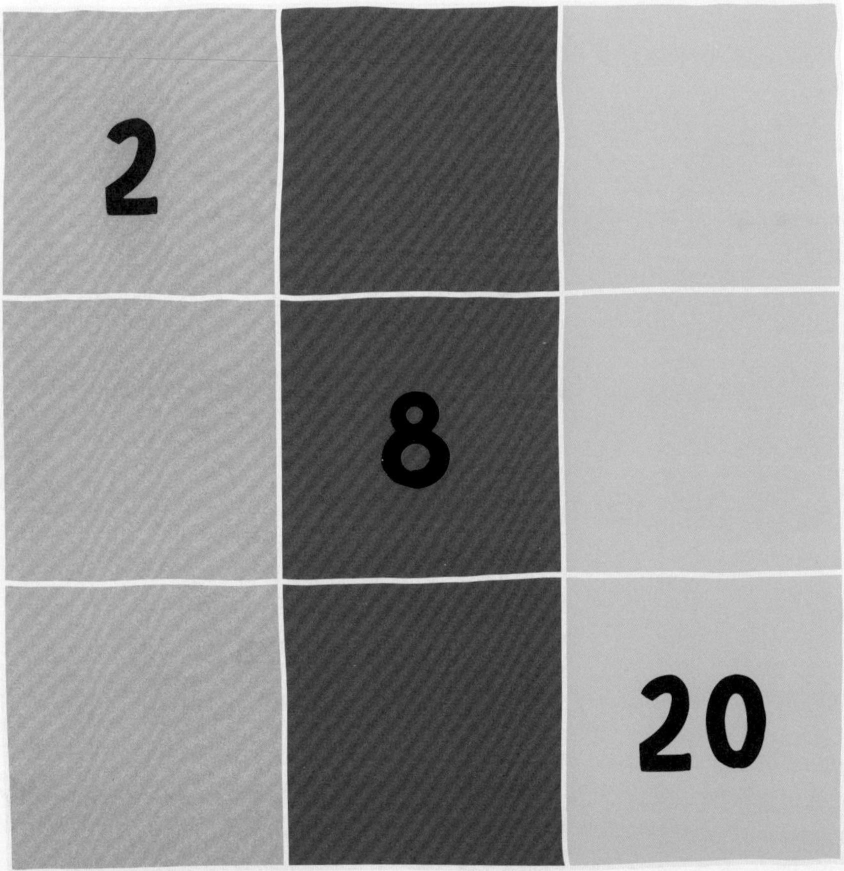

Dinosaur digits

See if you can fill in the missing numbers on these dinosaurs' spikes.

Spot the difference

Try to circle six differences in the right-hand picture.

17

Word count

Use any of these letters to make as many words as you can. You can use each letter only once.

....

....

....

....

Now, taking each letter to be worth the points shown below, see if you can find a six-letter word worth 50 points.

e:1 t:2 i:3 a:5 d:6 o:8 n:9 r:10 g:12

For example, 'tiger' would be worth 2+3+12+1+10=28 points.

Answer: .... (Clue: fiery monster)

Missing cookies

Each of these cookie jars can hold up to six cookies. The numbers on the shelves show the number of cookies that each shelf should hold. Draw the missing cookies in the jars.

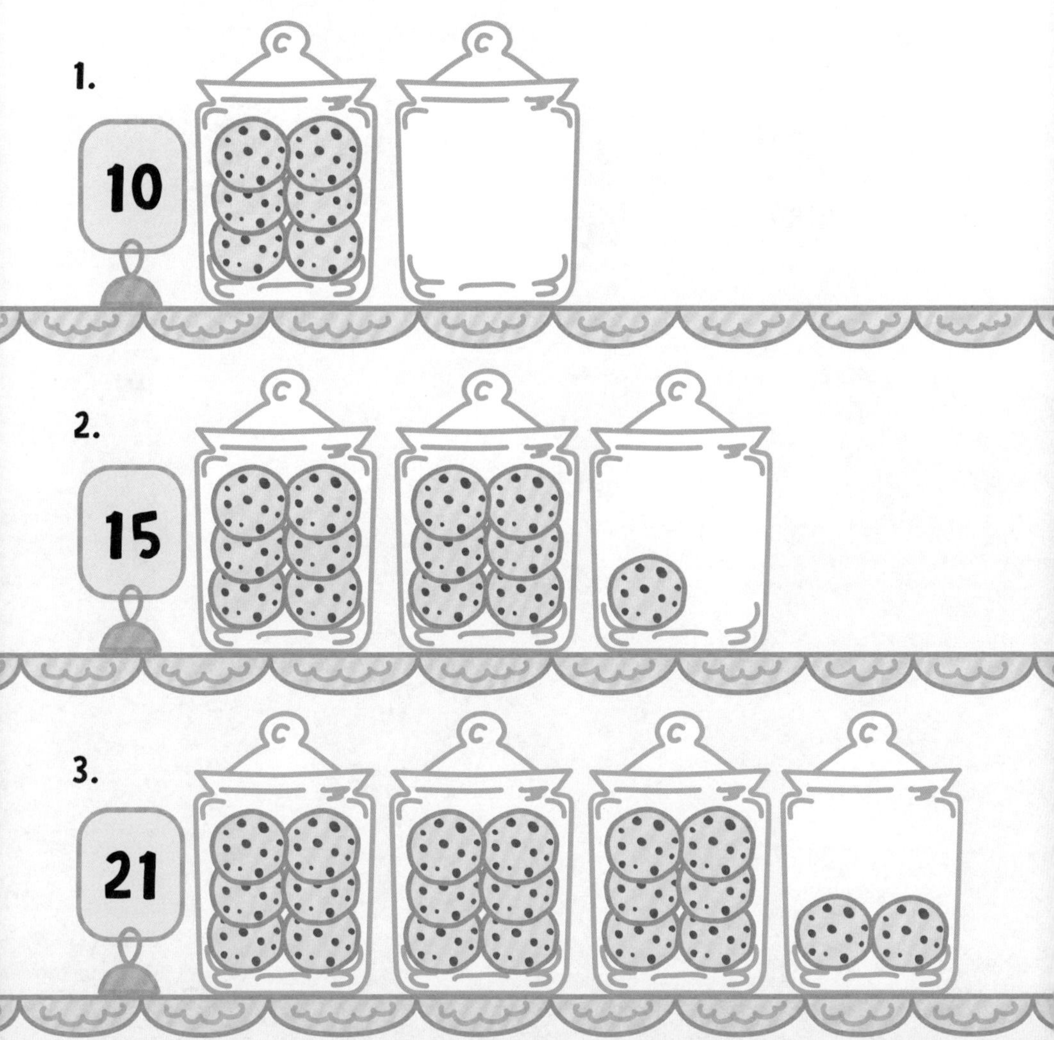

19

Necks letter

See if you can work out the letter sequences and fill in the empty patches on the giraffes' necks.

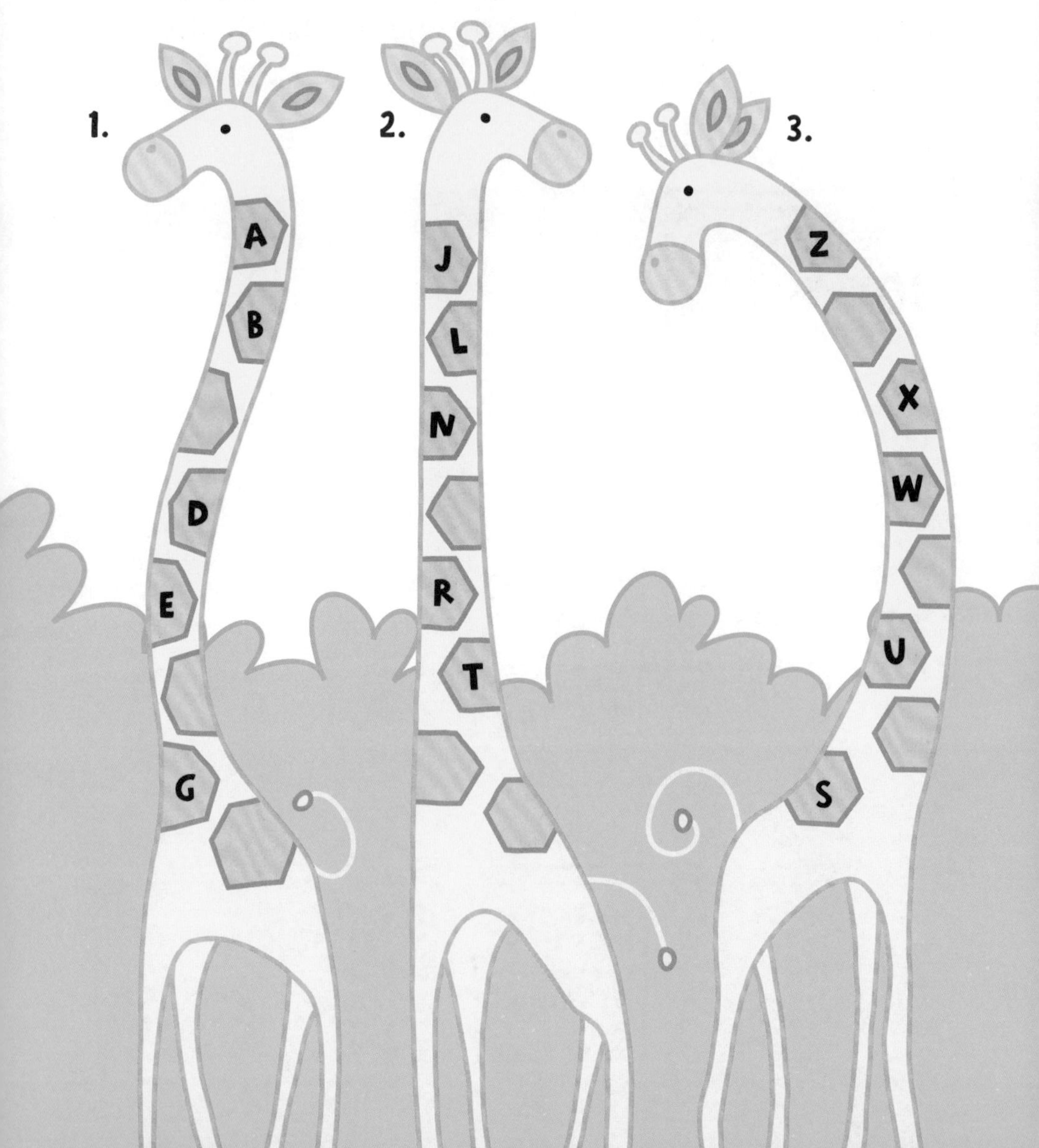

Mini-sudoku

Try to fill the grid below so that the numbers 1, 2, 3 and 4 appear in every line, column, and block of four squares. Here is an example.

3	4	1	2
1	2	3	4
4	3	2	1
2	1	4	3

		2	
	1		
1		4	
	3		

Crossword

ACROSS

1. a male lion's hair
2. the noise a lion makes
5. a chocolatey drink
7. a huge, hairy nut with sweet, white flesh
10. home, dwelling
11. used for washing
12. funny story or prank

DOWN

1. butterfly-like night insect
3. simple boat made of logs tied together
4. eight-legged sea creature
5. fabric or material
6. to entertain
8. small spots
9. friend, pal

Strawberry sundaes

Have a look at the ingredients in this sundae recipe, then answer the questions below.

to make two sundaes, you will need:
• 2 scoops of strawberry ice cream
• 2 scoops of vanilla ice cream
• 2 bowls of sliced strawberries
• 1 slice of sponge cake
• 2 dollops of whipped cream
• 3 teaspoons of chocolate sprinkles
• 2 wafers

1. How many sundaes can you make with this many teaspoons of chocolate sprinkles?

Answer:..........................

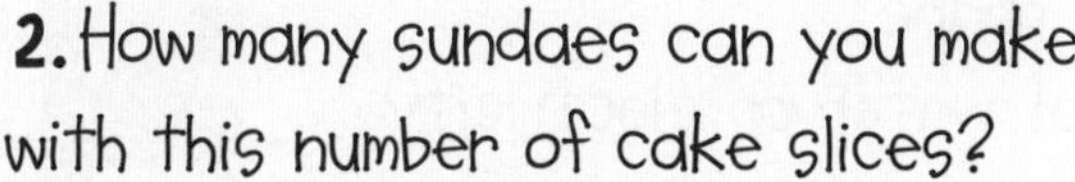

2. How many sundaes can you make with this number of cake slices?

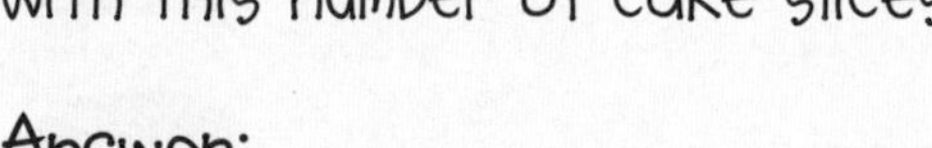

Answer:..........................

3. How many sundaes can you make with this many scoops of strawberry ice cream?

Answer:..........................

23

Confused words

People often mix up these pairs of similar-sounding words. For each pair, mark ✓ or ✗ to say whether the meanings given are correct.

1.	accept – to receive or agree to something except – not including	
2.	cereal – breakfast food serial – done in a series	
3.	dessert – a very dry area desert – an after-dinner treat	
4.	site – a certain place sight – the ability to see	
5.	currant – a dried grape current – a flow of water or electricity	
6.	coarse – a stage in a meal course – rough	
7.	break – a device for stopping a vehicle brake – to damage something, or split it up	

Number trains

Write the correct number or symbol onto each blank space to complete the number trains.

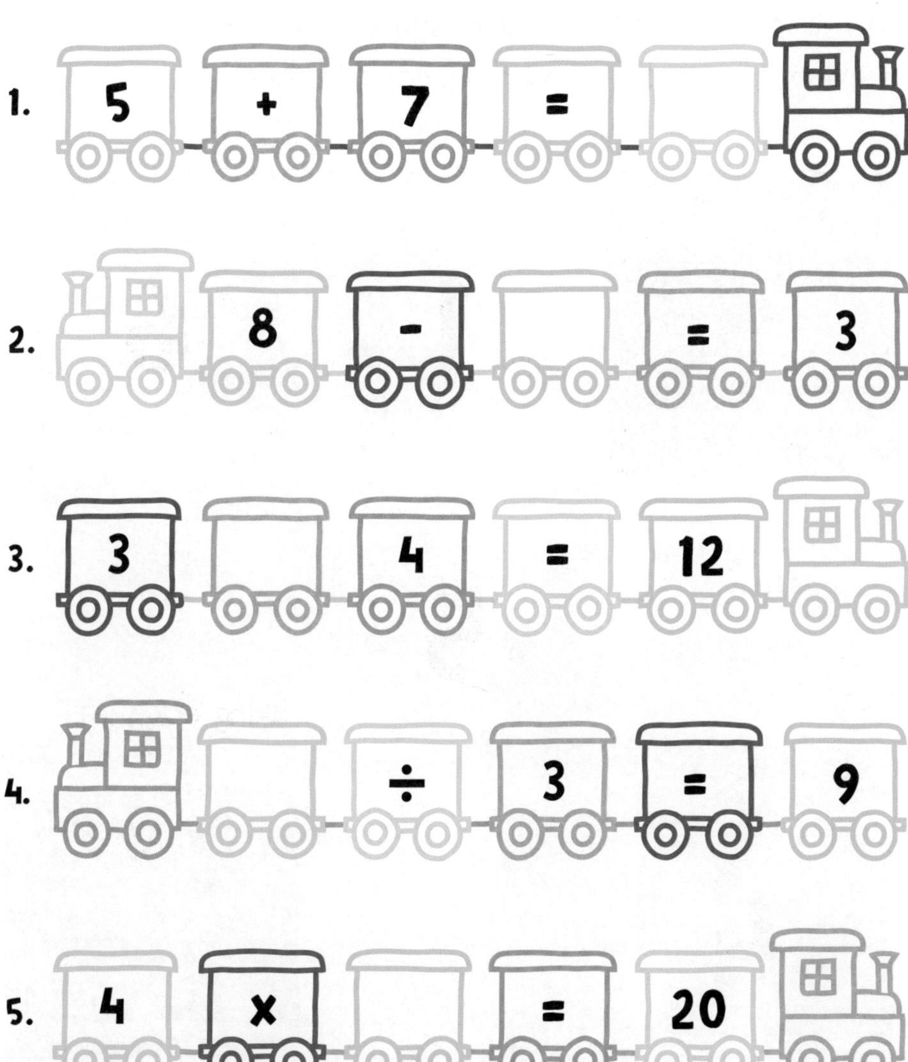

Magic square

In a magic square, the numbers in every row, column and diagonal add up to the same total. Write a number in each empty box of this magic square so that the numbers in every row, column and diagonal add up to 15.

Avoid the asteroids

Find the path the alien must take to fly his spaceship safely through the asteroid field back to his home planet.

27

Mini-sudoku

Try to fill the grid below so that the numbers 1, 2, 3 and 4 appear in every line, column, and block of four squares. Here is an example.

3	4	1	2
1	2	3	4
4	3	2	1
2	1	4	3

1	3	2	
	4	1	2

How many birds?

How many birds can you see below?

Answer: ....

What goes where?

Try to fill the grid below so that each of the four pictures appears in every line, column, and block of four squares. Here is an example.

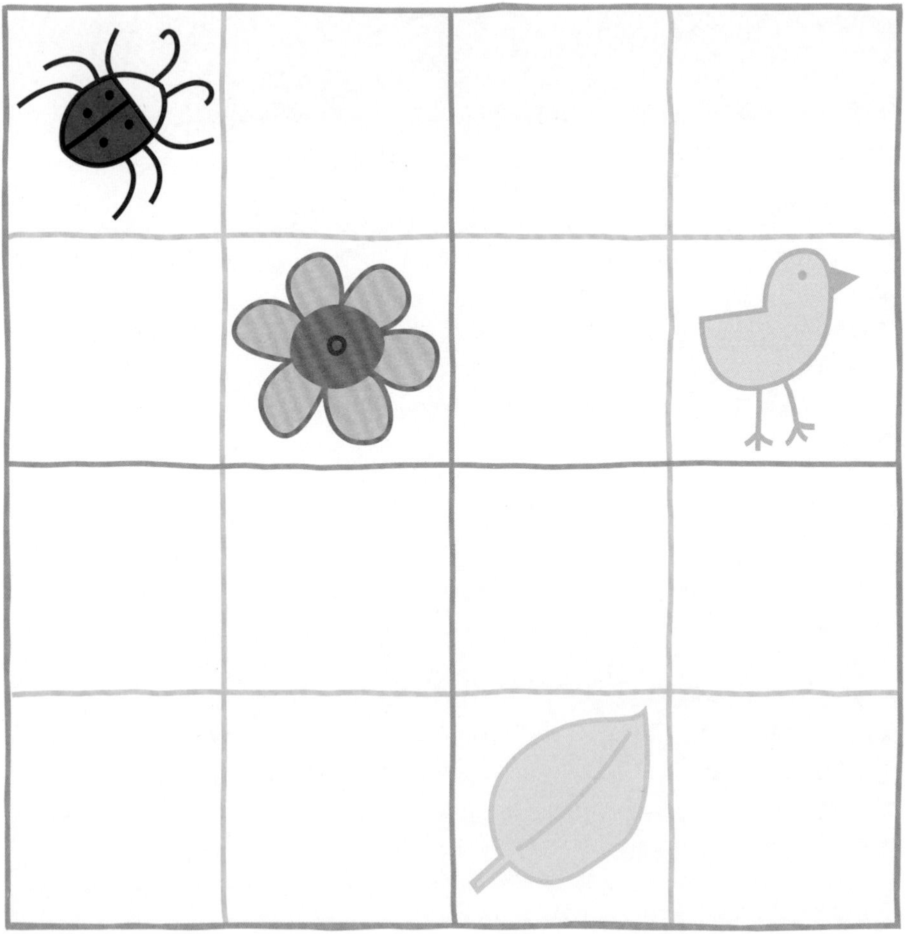

Picture letter

In this puzzle, pictures or symbols stand for words. See if you can figure out what the letter says.

Counting triangles

How many triangles can you count here?

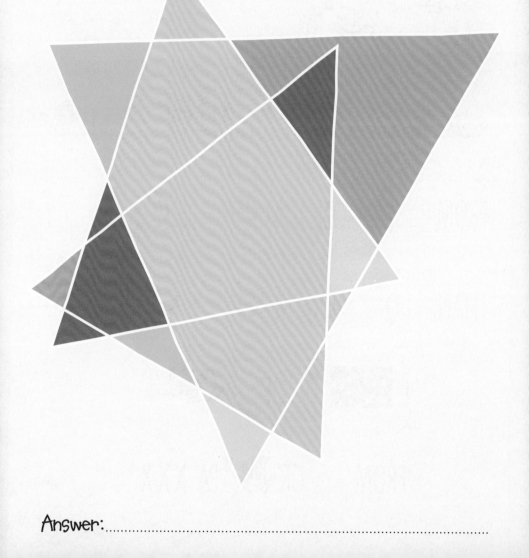

Answer: ....

Toy box

Look at the toys for one minute, then cover the pictures and try to answer the questions below.

1. Is the doll's dress red, green or blue?

....

2. How many teddy bears are there?

....

3. Does the ball have stripes?

....

4. Which toy is on the right of the toy box?

....

5. Which letters are on the wooden blocks?

....

6. Is the train facing left or right?

....

33

Honeycomb hexagons

Fit the words into the honeycomb. Each word starts in a bright yellow cell and winds clockwise around an orange cell.

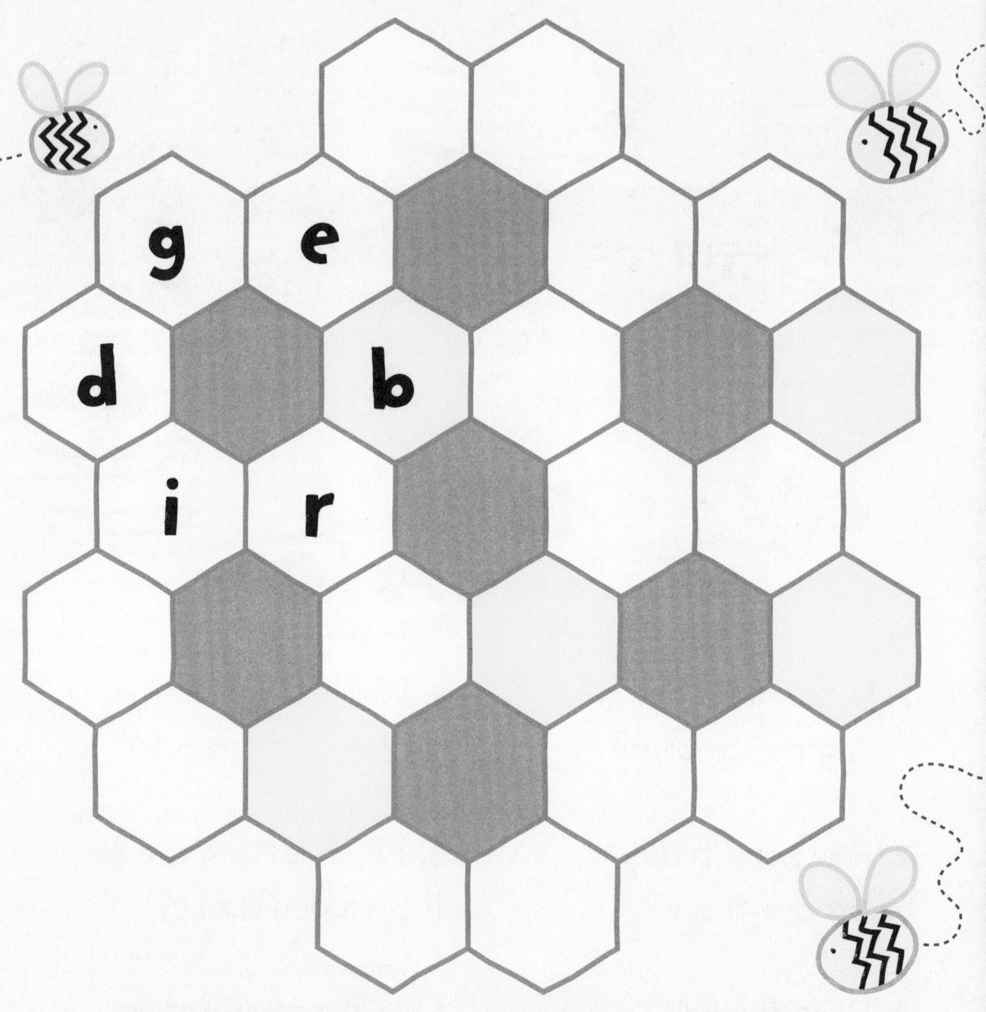

beetle hotels ~~bridge~~ grotto

better empire toffee

Rupanapi Island

Rupanapi Island has two lines of mysterious old statues, but some of them have fallen down. Draw arrows showing which of the fallen statues at the bottom of the page should go in each gap.

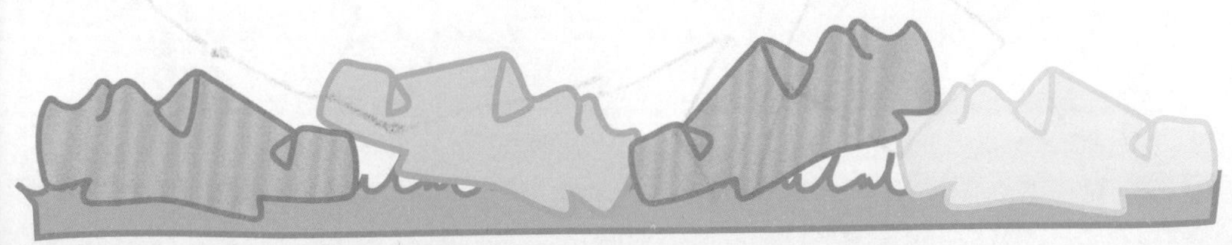

Under the sea

Join up the dots to discover what lies on the ocean bed.

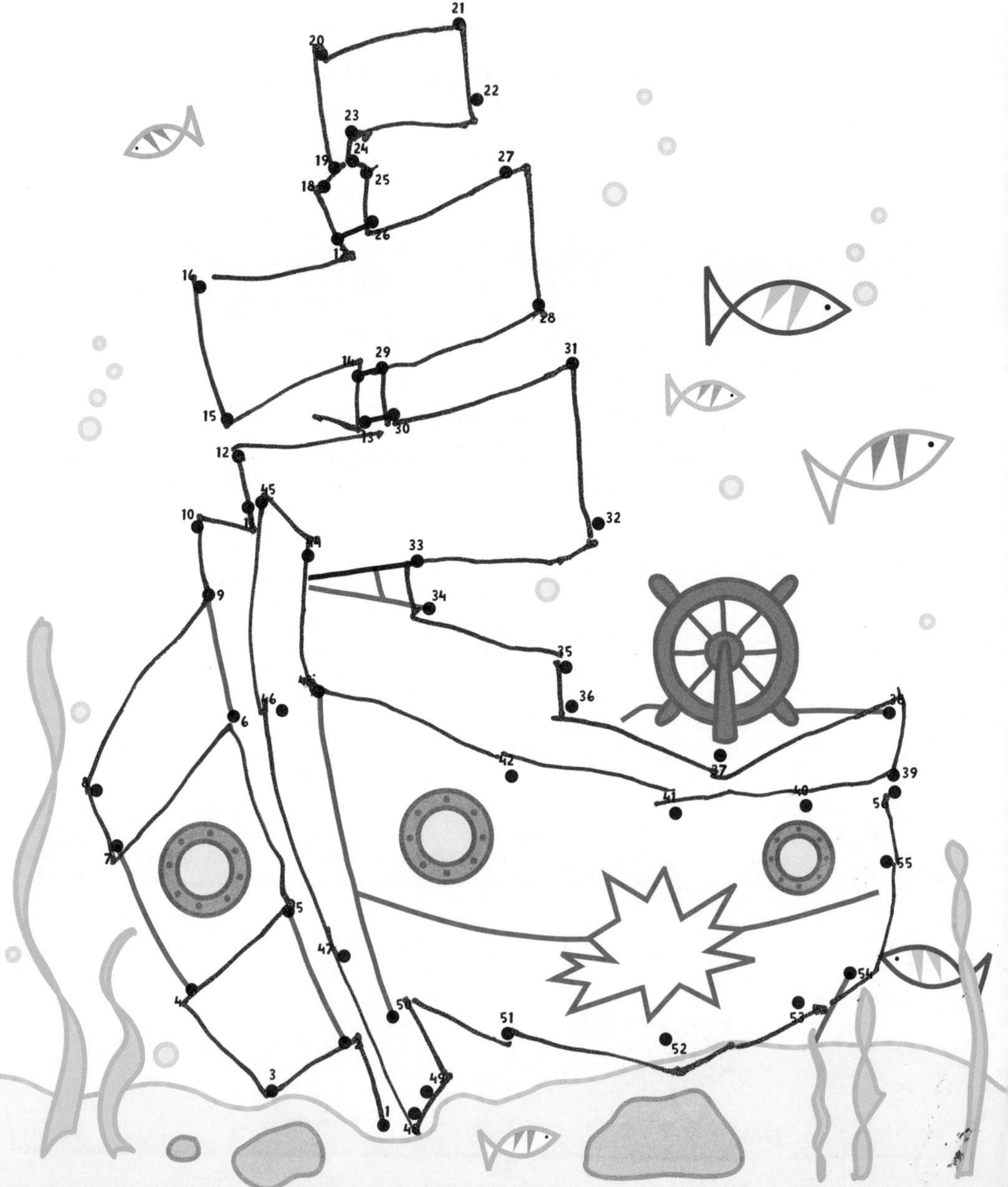

Find the dogs

See if you can find the dog breeds below in the grid.
Their names may be written in any direction.

R	E	L	D	O	O	P	N	L	L	H	C	W
O	I	L	A	B	B	R	C	H	R	W	K	C
U	E	E	L	B	T	U	N	G	H	O	C	A
G	N	I	M	B	R	L	L	Y	C	H	S	O
H	A	E	A	O	D	A	B	L	A	C	Y	O
C	D	N	T	I	B	S	D	L	D	W	D	U
O	T	H	I	K	I	E	S	O	W	O	B	D
L	A	O	A	S	O	R	A	S	R	H	G	O
L	E	I	N	A	P	S	R	E	K	C	O	C
I	R	B	E	A	G	L	E	B	N	S	O	A
E	G	R	E	Y	H	O	U	N	D	W	D	R
P	A	A	D	O	C	B	W	S	I	R	P	I
L	G	G	E	N	T	H	D	K	D	E	S	D

cocker spaniel, rough collie, greyhound, labrador, poodle,
great dane, chow chow, dalmatian, bulldog, beagle

37 Confused countries

See if you can unscramble these country names.

1. yuTrek

....

2. yenGram

....

3. carFen

....

4. groutlaP

....

5. Chain

....

6. Greta Brainit

....

7. oxMice

....

8. taStes Untied

....

9. oldPan

....

10. Shout ifAcar

....

Hidden picture

Shade in the shapes that have a blue dot to show a place a knight might call home.

39 Directions

Where will the three cars end up if they follow the directions below?

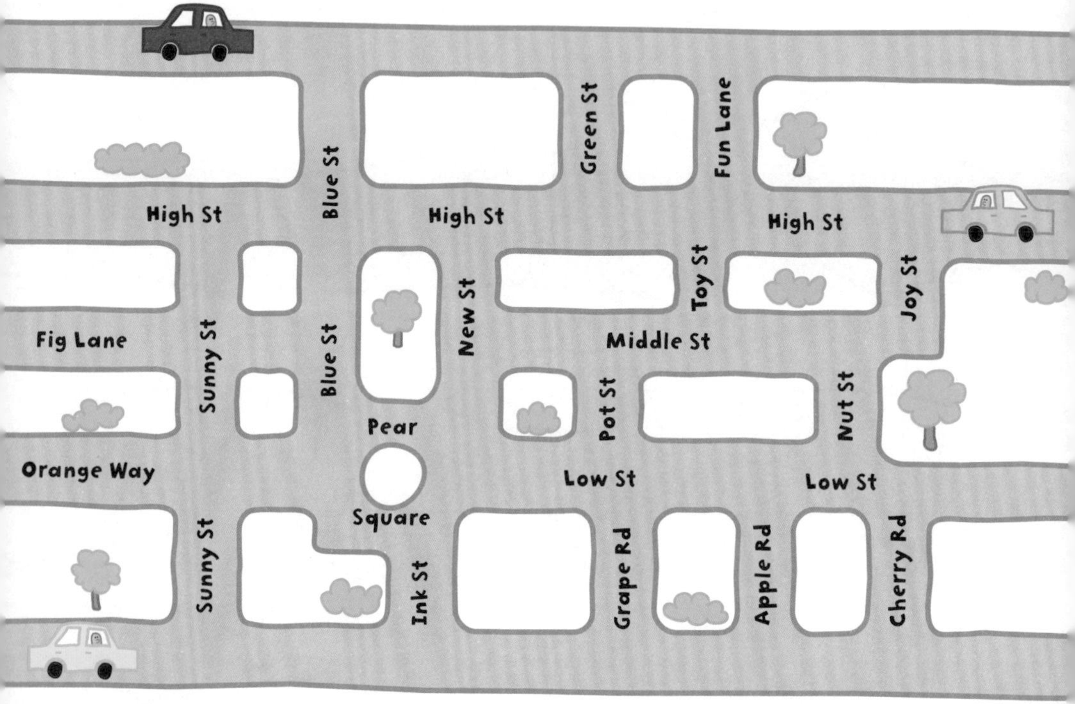

1st right, 2nd right, 1st left, 2nd left, 3rd left

....

2nd left, 1st right, 1st left, 1st right, 1st left

....

3rd left, 2nd right, 1st left, 1st left, 1st right

....

Copy Hoppy

Copy the picture of Hoppy the rabbit by looking closely at what is in each square.

Triangle art

Shade in the triangles below to see a picture of a world-famous landmark.

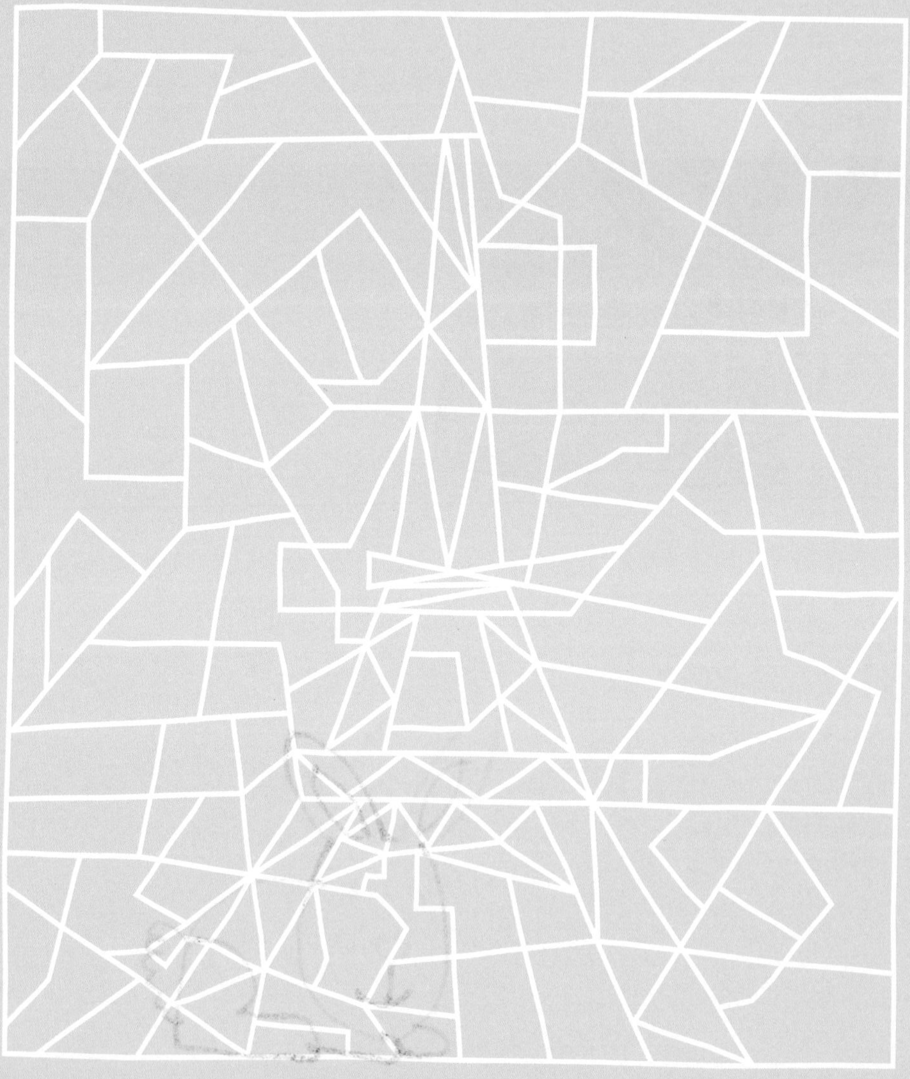

Birds on a wire

The little blue birds want to sit next to each other on the wire. The big yellow birds do, too. The birds can hop over each other one at a time. Try to help them get together in three hops. Draw in the position of the birds after each hop, on the wires below.

1.

2.

3.

Shredded words

The words below have been broken in two. Find their missing endings, then draw a line to join them.

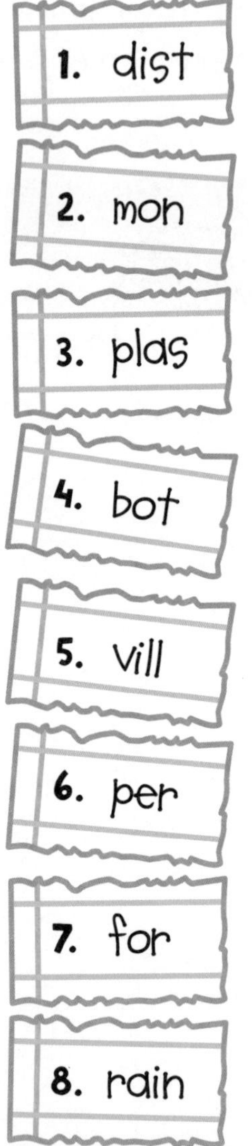

Apple picking

These apples must be picked in order: the apple with the lowest value first, and the one with the highest value last.

- Draw an X over the apples to be picked first and last.
- Draw a ✓ over the apples to be picked 6th and 10th.
- Draw a circle over the apples to be picked 3rd and 13th.

45 Sticker selection

Amy and Ben are choosing from these stickers. Amy wants the red ones, and Ben wants the star-shaped ones. Draw a circle around the stickers Amy wants, and an X through the stickers Ben would like.

1. How many stickers are wanted by both?

....

2. How many stickers do neither of them want?

....

Dog show

Which dog should be awarded which prize? Write 1st, 2nd or 3rd on the trophies next to each dog. Some of the spaces have already been filled in for you.

Rhyming stones

Help Philippe the sheep get across the river by drawing a path between stepping stones with words that all rhyme.

Jigwords

Finish fitting the letter patterns shown below into the grid to reveal the name of a creepy-crawly in each row.

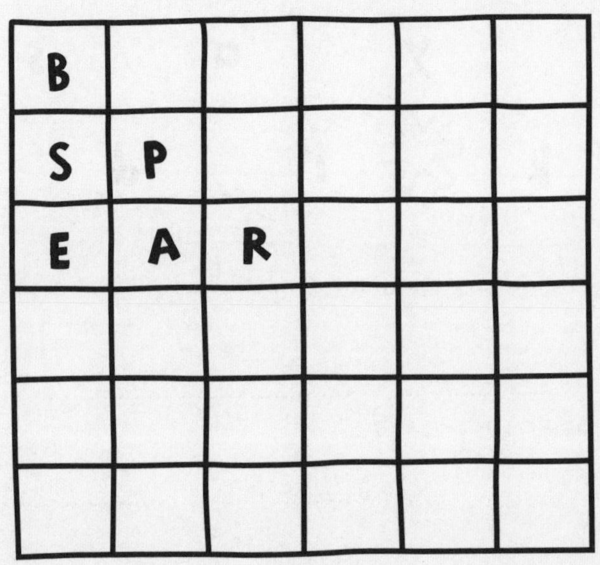

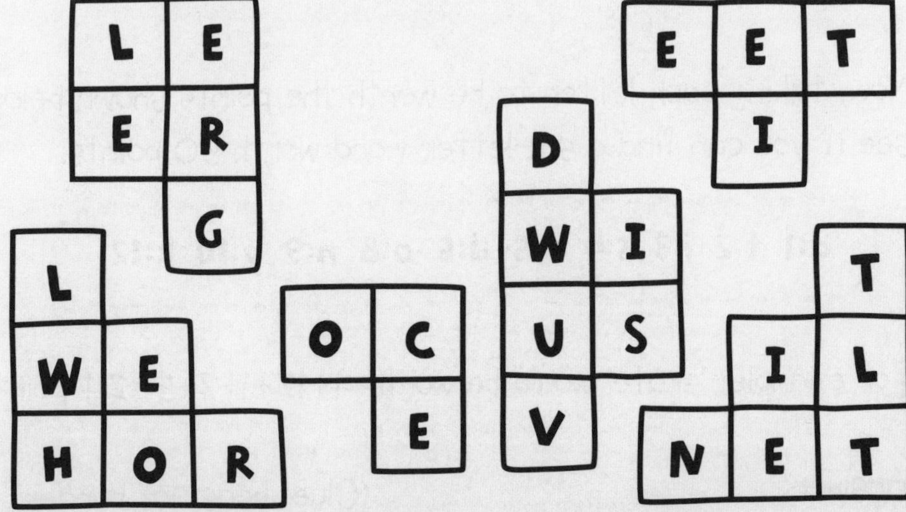

Word count

Use any of these letters to make as many words as you can. You can use each letter only once.

a y o s t

n k i d e

....

....

....

....

Now, taking each letter to be worth the points shown below, see if you can find a six-letter word worth 50 points.

a:1 t:2 i:3 s:4 e:5 d:6 o:8 n:9 y:10 k:12

For example, 'skate' would be worth 4+12+1+2+5=24 points.

Answer: .... (Clue: beast of burden)

Tricky T-shirts

Use these clues to draw the right design on each T-shirt:

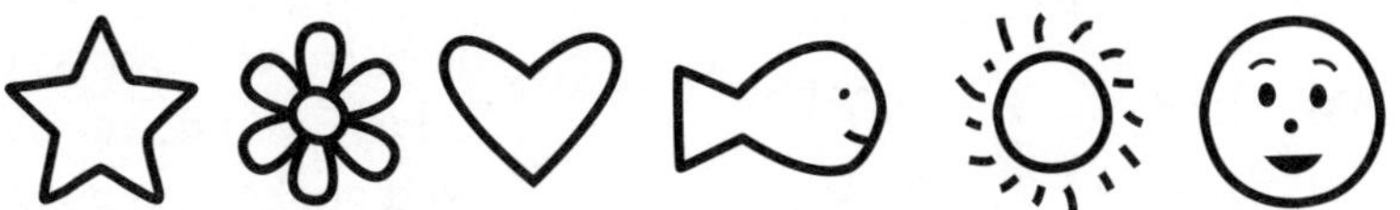

- The star design is between the flower design and the face design.
- The heart design is below the flower design.
- The sun design is to the left of both the fish design and the heart design.

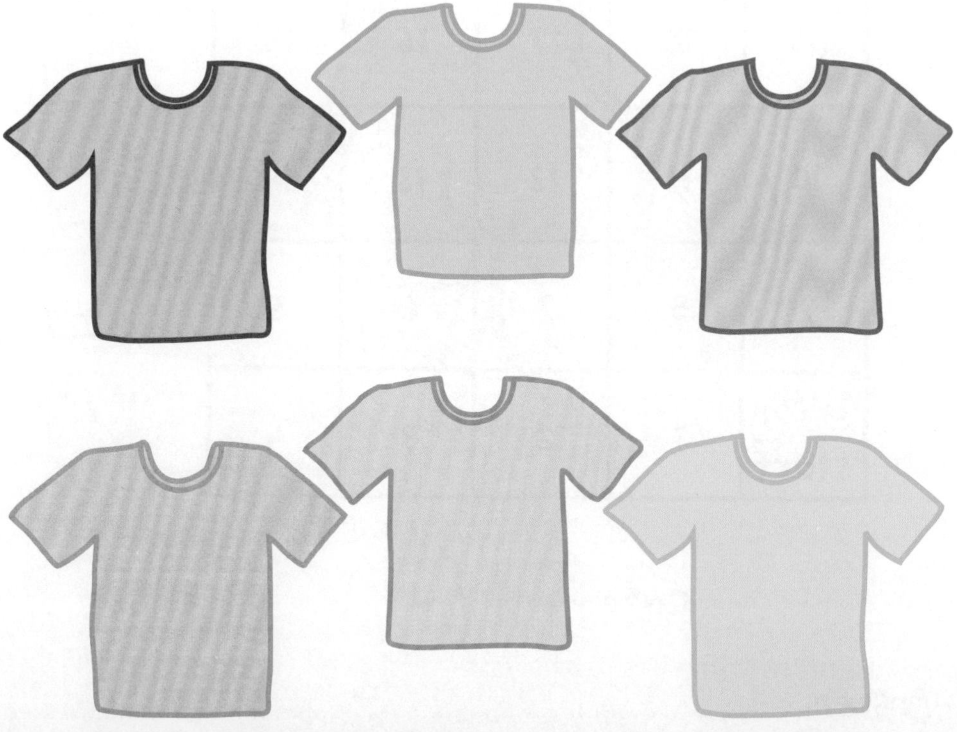

51

Snake and ladders

Alfie, Beth and Cate have just played snakes and ladders. Look at their dice rolls to find out who got farthest.

Rules: move the number of squares rolled on your dice. If you land on a ladder, you go up it; and on a snake you go down.

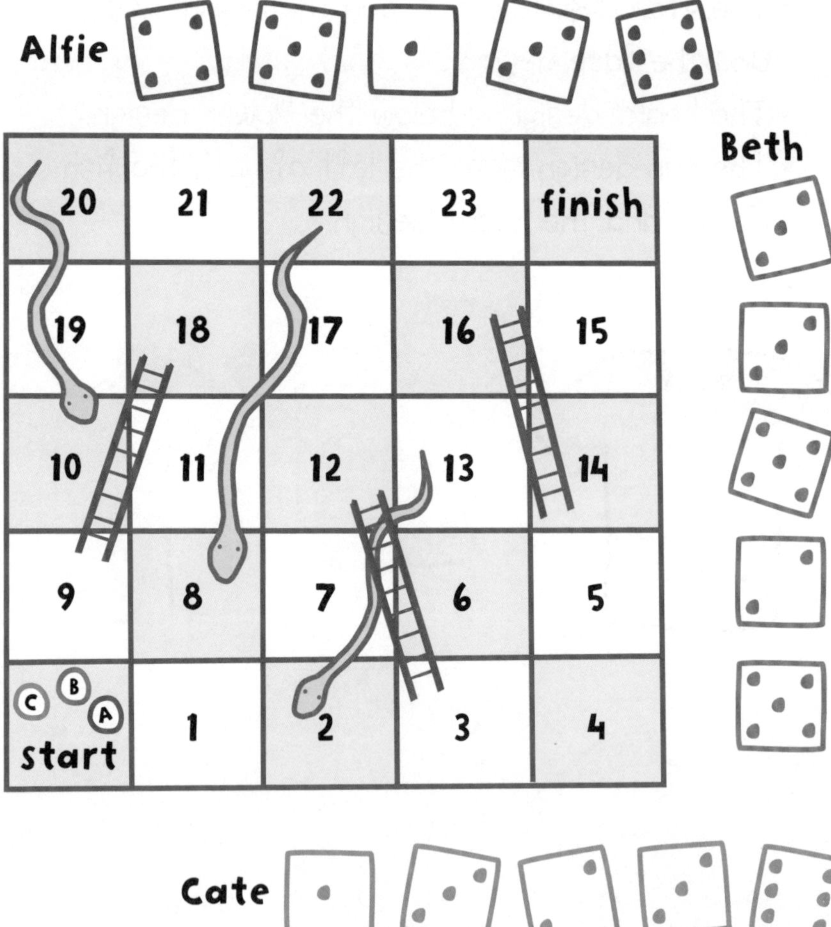

Answer: ....

3-D shapes

See if you can draw lines connecting the flat, unfolded nets with the 3-D shapes that can be made from them.

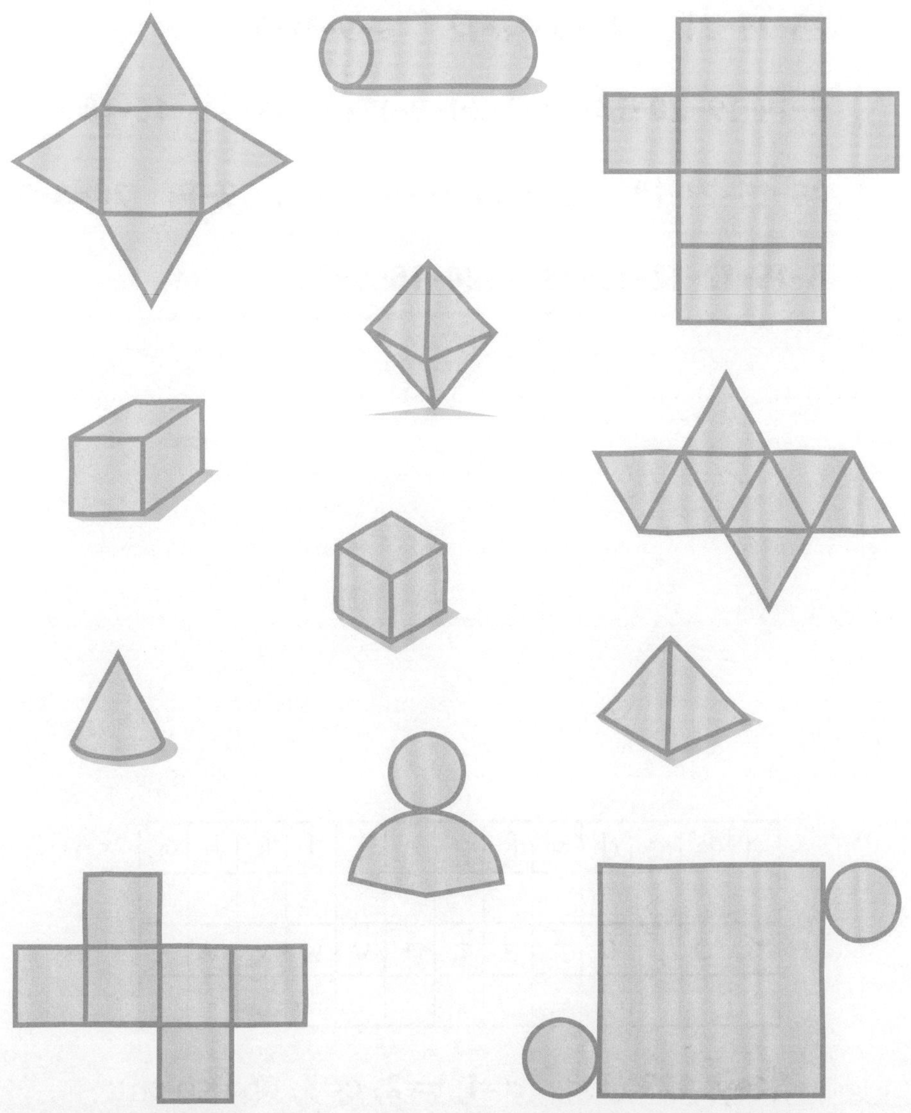

Secret code

This secret spy message has been written in code.
Use the key below to decode the message.

25-15-21 23-9-12-12 6-9-14-4

9-14-19-20-18-21-3-20-9-15-14-19 6-15-18

25-15-21-18 13-9-19-19-9-15-14 9-14 20-8-5

8-15-12-12-15-23 20-18-5-5.

a	b	c	d	e	f	g	h	i	j	k	l	m
n	o	p	q	r	s	t	u	v	w	x	y	z

Key: **123** Code a=**1**, b=**2**, c=**3**, and so on

Pasta pieces

How many pieces of pasta can you count here?

Coconut palm

Join the dots in number order to give this coconut palm tree its leaves.

Pirate Pete

See if you can circle six differences in the right-hand picture of Pirate Pete.

Picture crossword

Take the first letter of each picture clue in the big grid to find the right letters to fill in the little grid.

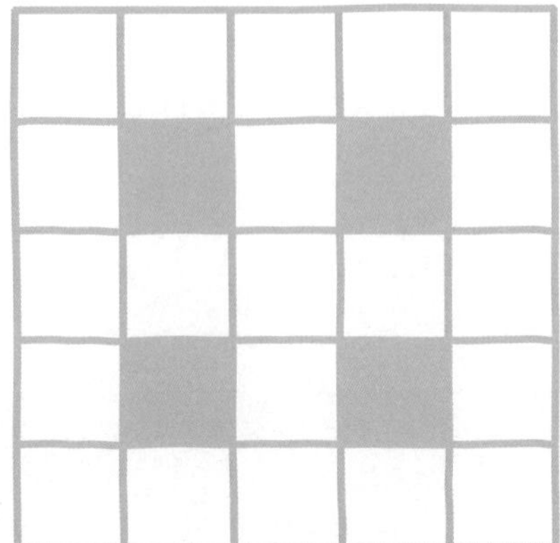

Cross country

Arrange the six country names in the grid below so that the red circles spell out a country famous for maple syrup.

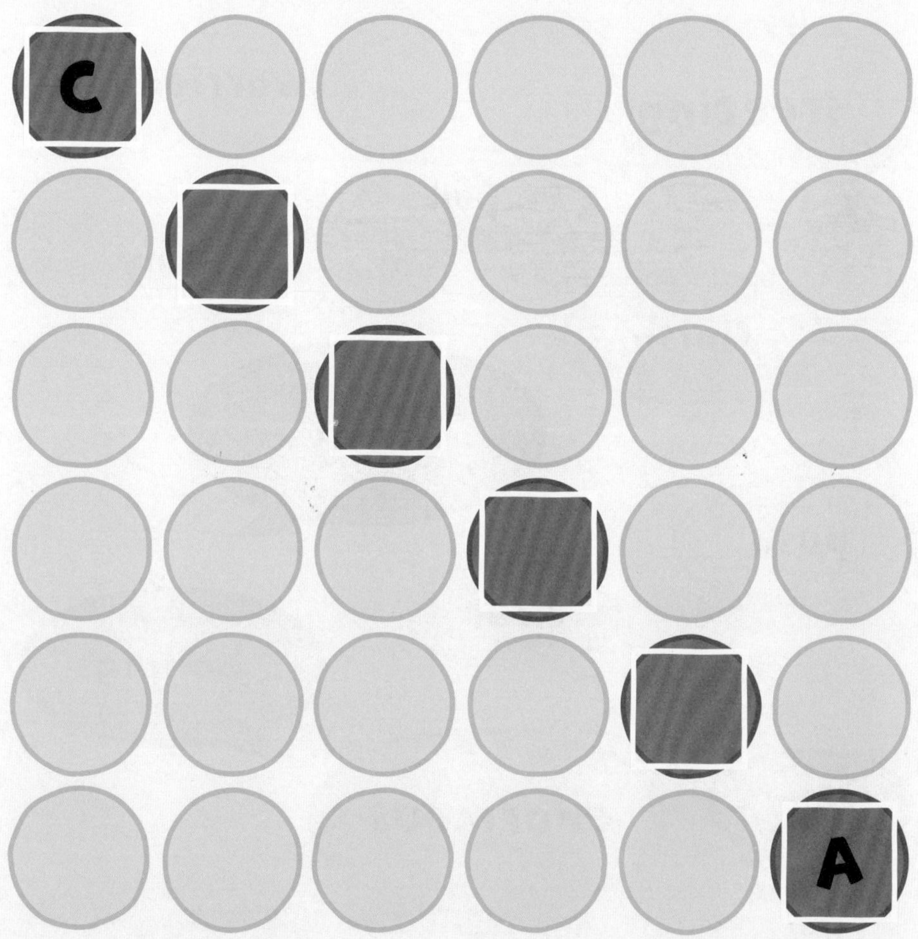

GUYANA CYPRUS RUSSIA

MONACO RWANDA LATVIA

Opposite pairs

All but one of these words can be paired up with another one, with the opposite meaning. Circle the word on its own.

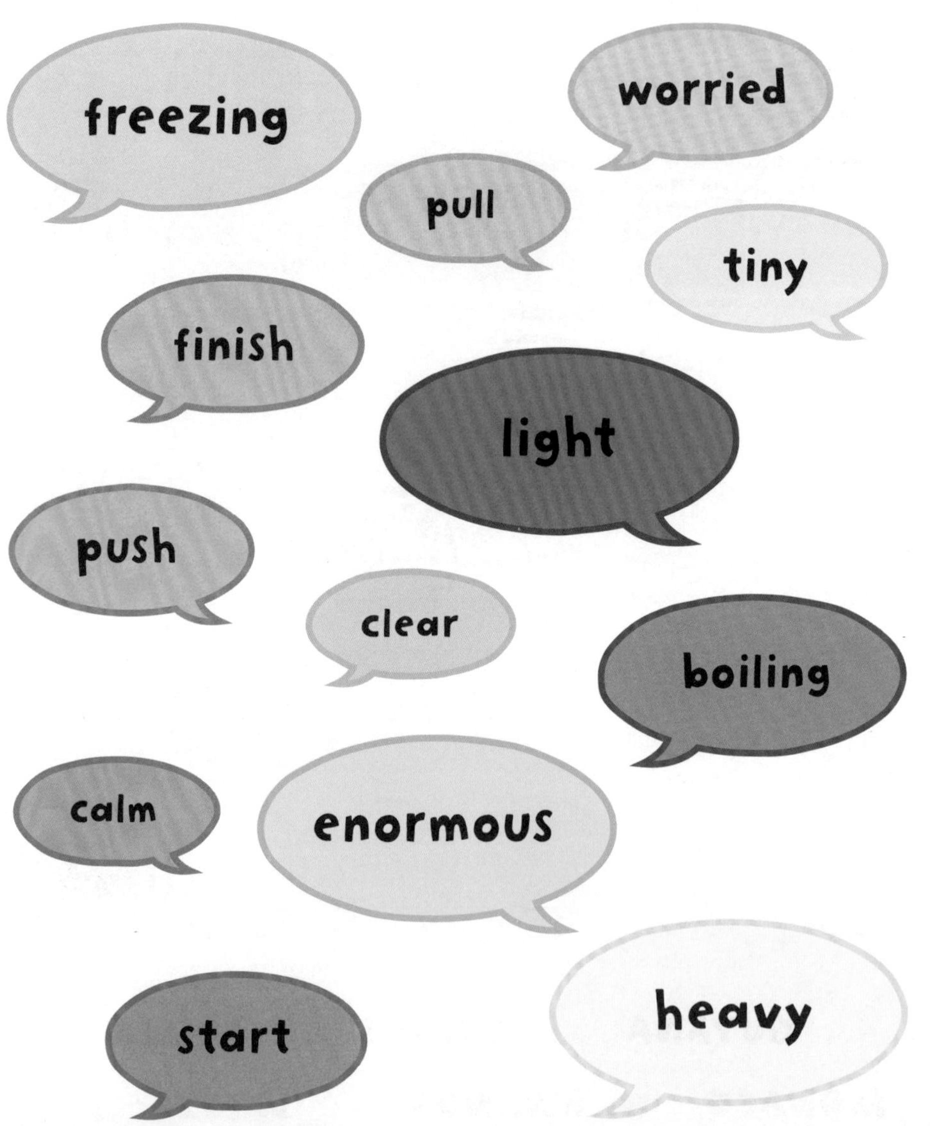

Cross-sum

Place numbers in the grid so that each row and column adds up to the total shown in the arrow. Each number in a row or column must be different.

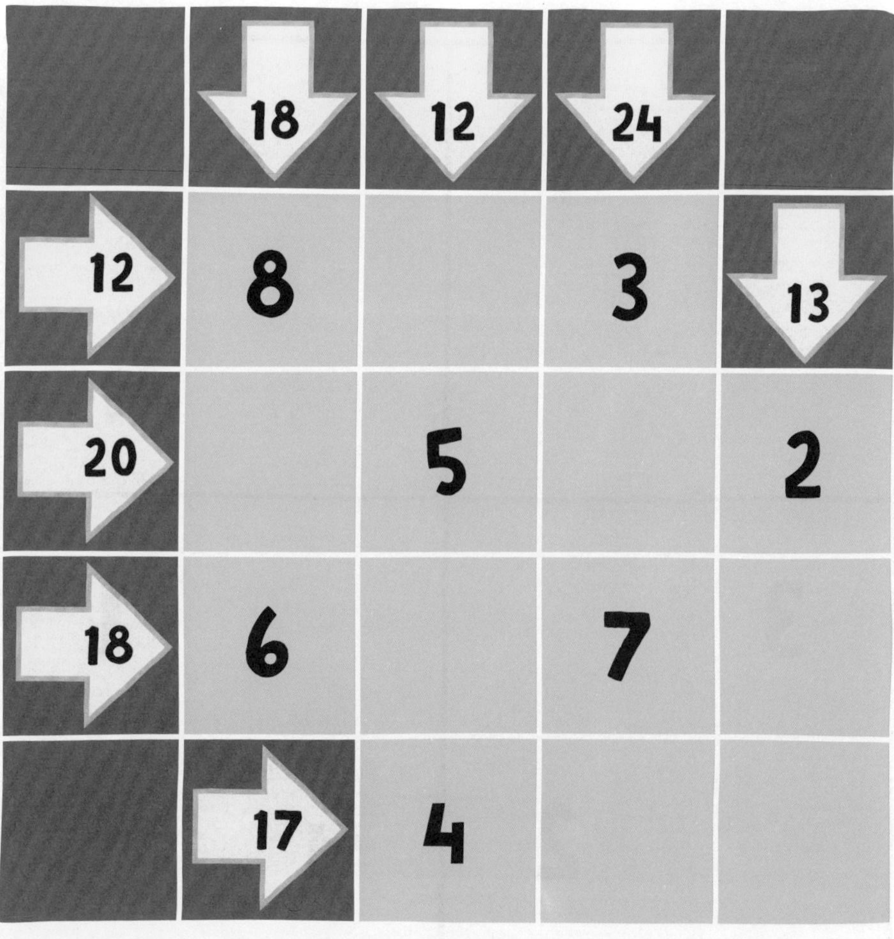

Mini-sudoku

Try to fill the grid below so that the numbers 1, 2, 3 and 4 appear in every line, column, and block of four squares. Here is an example.

3	4	1	2
1	2	3	4
4	3	2	1
2	1	4	3

	1		
			4
3			1
	2	4	

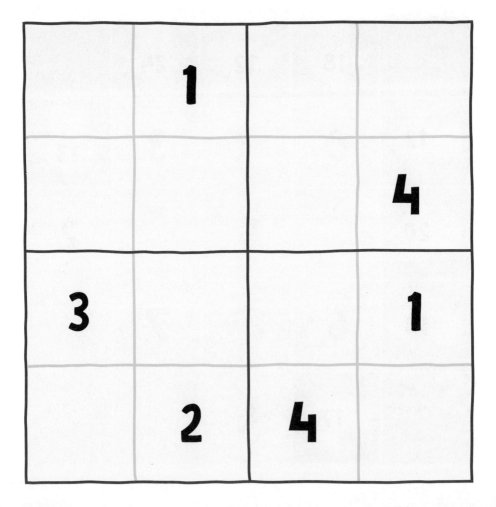

Back to the start

Find out which set of instructions was used to draw the shape, then circle the dot where the drawing began.

1. right 3, down 2, right 1, down 1, left 1, down 2, left 1, up 3, left 2, up 1, right 3, up 1, left 2, up 1

2. left 3, up 1, right 3, up 1, left 2, up 1, right 3, down 3, right 1, down 1, left 1, down 2, left 1, up 2

3. left 1, up 2, left 3, down 1, right 2, down 1, left 3, down 1, right 3, down 2, right 1, up 2, right 1, up 1

Spider's web

Fit the spider words into the web so that they spiral into the middle – the first letters are given. At the end, the shaded parts will spell out the name of a very big spider.

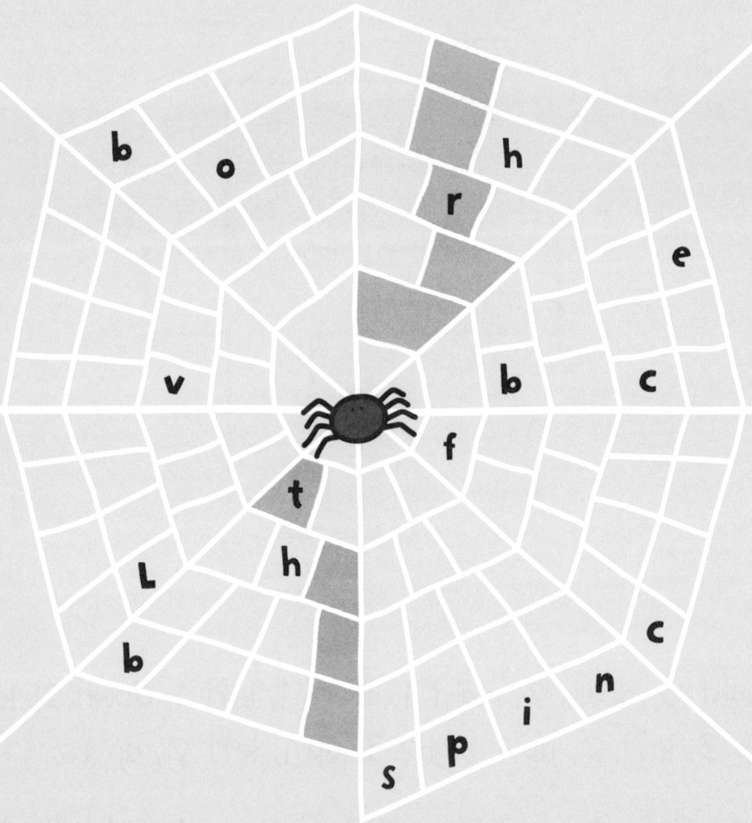

b o h r e v b c f t h L b c n i p s

~~spin~~
banana spider
black widow
cobweb
Little Miss Muffet
blue blood
eight legs
fangs
hairy
hunters
climb
orbweaver
redback
trap
venom

64 Fairytale mix-up

See if you can unscramble the mixed-up names of the fairytale characters below.

1. OLDSKICLOG

....

2. TILTEL DER GNIRID DOOH

....

3. OWNS HEWIT

....

4. SHANEL DAN TRELEG

....

5. ELLIDANCER

....

6. GLEESNIP BUYTEA

....

Missing shapes

Circle the shape that completes each sequence.

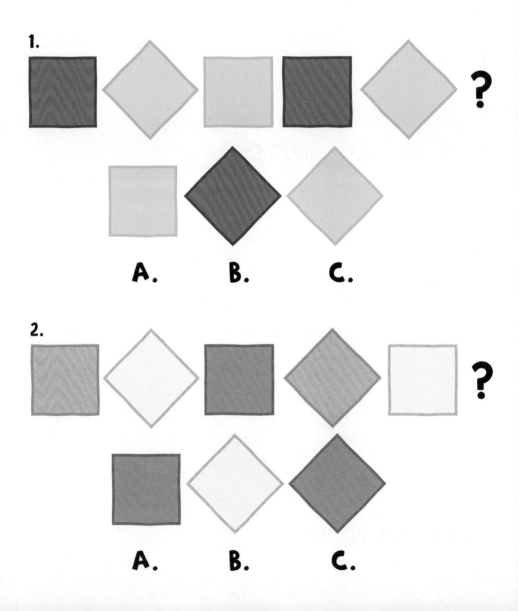

1. ?

A. B. C.

2. ?

A. B. C.

Secret code

This secret spy message has been written in code.
Use the key below to decode the message.

TOP SECRET

Nffu nf bu uif sbjmxbz tubujpo bu tjy qn po Uivstebz. J xjmm dbssz sfe sptft.

....

....

....

....

....

....

a	b	c	d	e	f	g	h	i	j	k	l	m
n	o	p	q	r	s	t	u	v	w	x	y	z

Key: +1 Code a=b, b=c, c=d, and so on to z=a

Have a heart

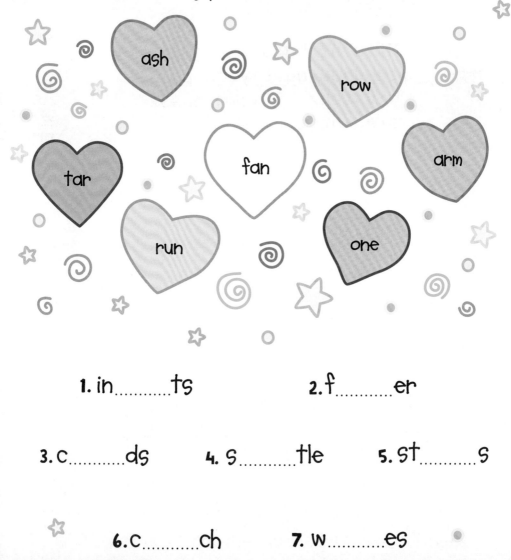

The words at the bottom all need three-letter 'hearts' in their middles to make them whole. Write the correct heart word in each gap to make whole new words.

1. in..........ts
2. f..........er
3. c..........ds
4. s..........tle
5. st..........s
6. c..........ch
7. w..........es

68 Pirate Pete's treasure

Follow the instructions on Pirate Pete's treasure map to find out where he has buried his precious loot, then mark the spot with an 'X'.

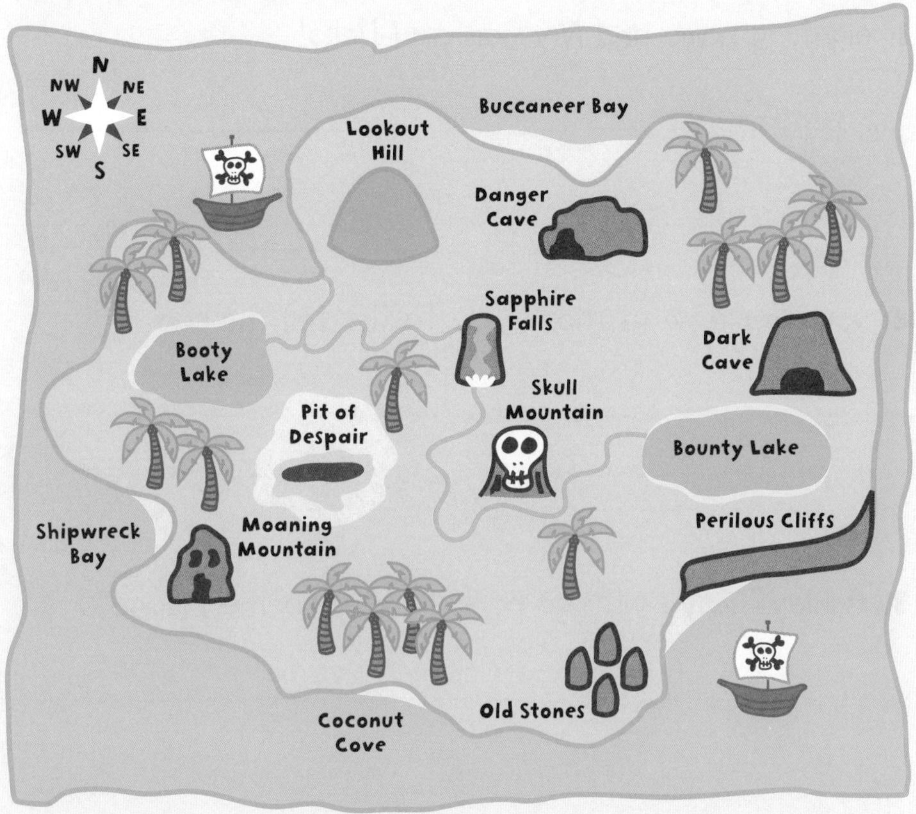

Land your ship at the mouth of the river. Walk east till you see a cave to your north. Then head southeast until you reach a lake. Now head west until you see a mountain to the southwest. Then you must cross a river to your south, to reach a single tree. Now walk west until that mountain is to the north. Finally, head south until you stand between four and four. Then dig deep, and the treasure will be yours!

69 Crazy talk

Try to rewrite these mixed-up sentences so that their words and punctuation are in the right order.

1. eight. is name and My Sam am I Hello!

....

....

2. you Please me station? way to the tell the can

....

....

3. Ashley? may I with go park to play to the Please

....

....

4. did you really cool. your shoes? Where They're buy

....

....

Alphablocks

Number the blocks at the bottom in alphabetical order, then copy their shapes into the grid to make a pattern.

1.	2.	3.	4.	5.
6.	7.	8.	9.	10.
11.	12.	13.	14.	15.

Pizza pieces

Which is the missing piece of the pizza?

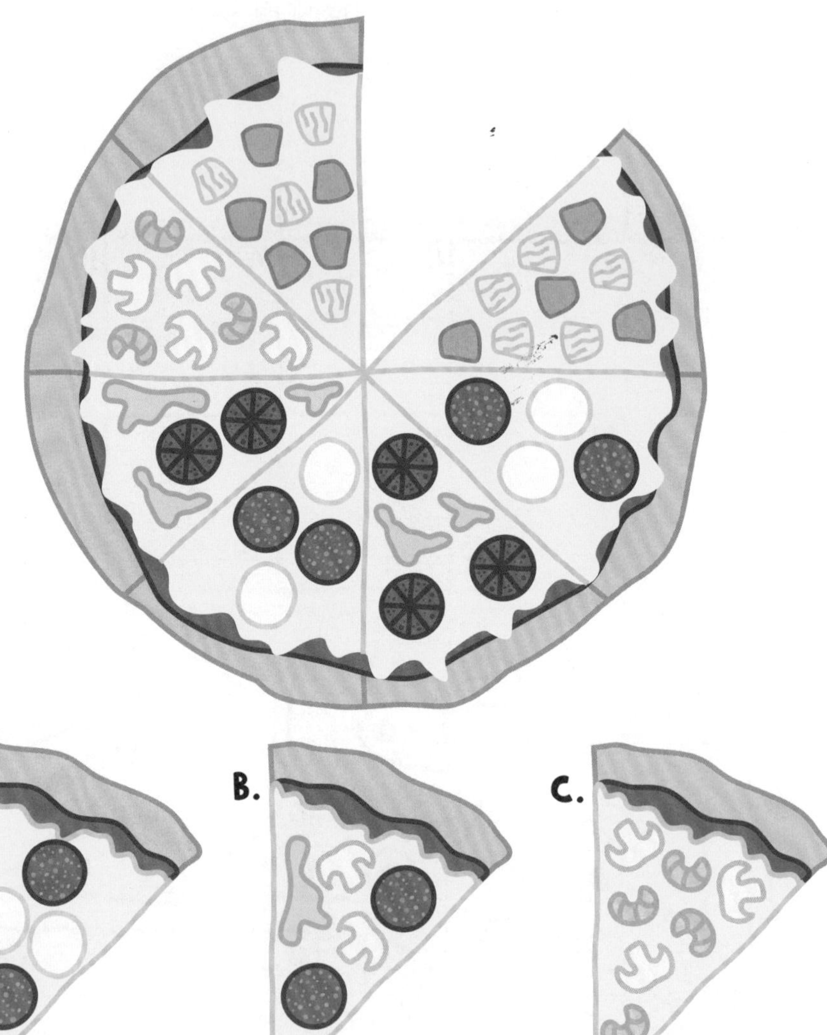

A.

B.

C.

Answer: ....

How many penguins?

Which iceberg has the most penguins on it?

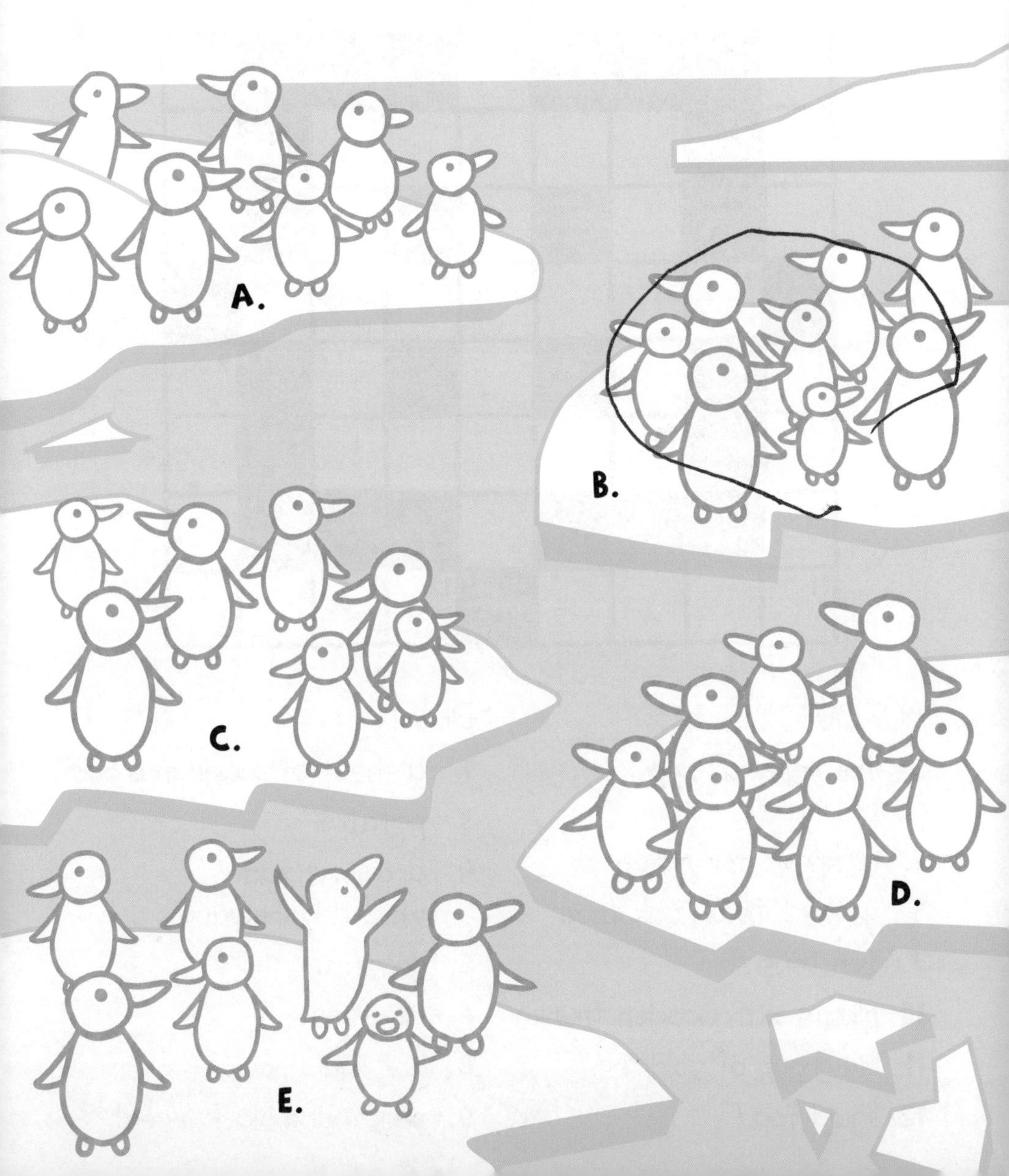

Crossword

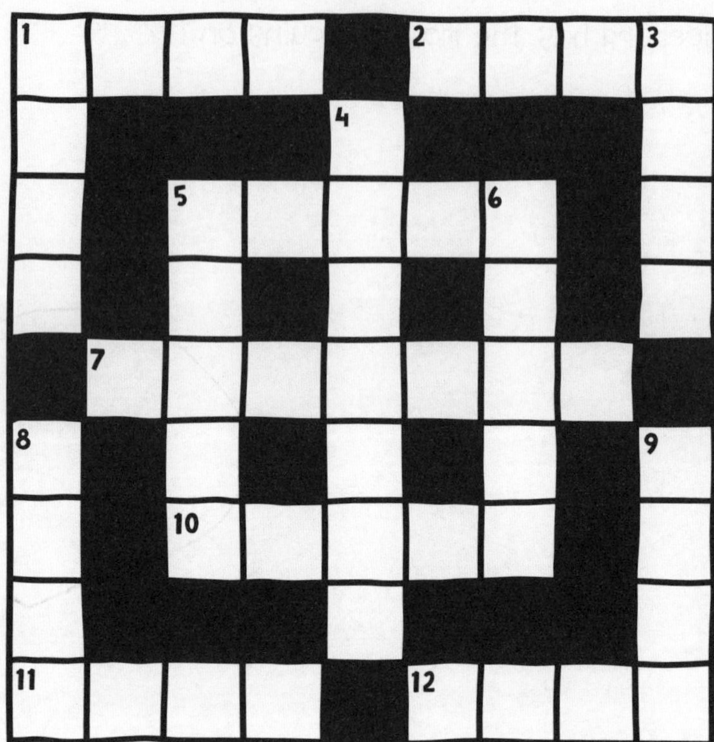

ACROSS

1. the noise a happy cat makes
2. nickname for police
5. grows into an oak tree
7. ten tens
10. plants with wooden trunks
11. big group of soldiers
12. liquid food

DOWN

1. a sheet of paper in a book
3. potato
4. drawings made while daydreaming
5. grown-up
6. requires
8. hot liquid rock
9. yellow and black insect

Find the beetle

Find the one beetle on this page that isn't one of a pair, and draw a circle around it.

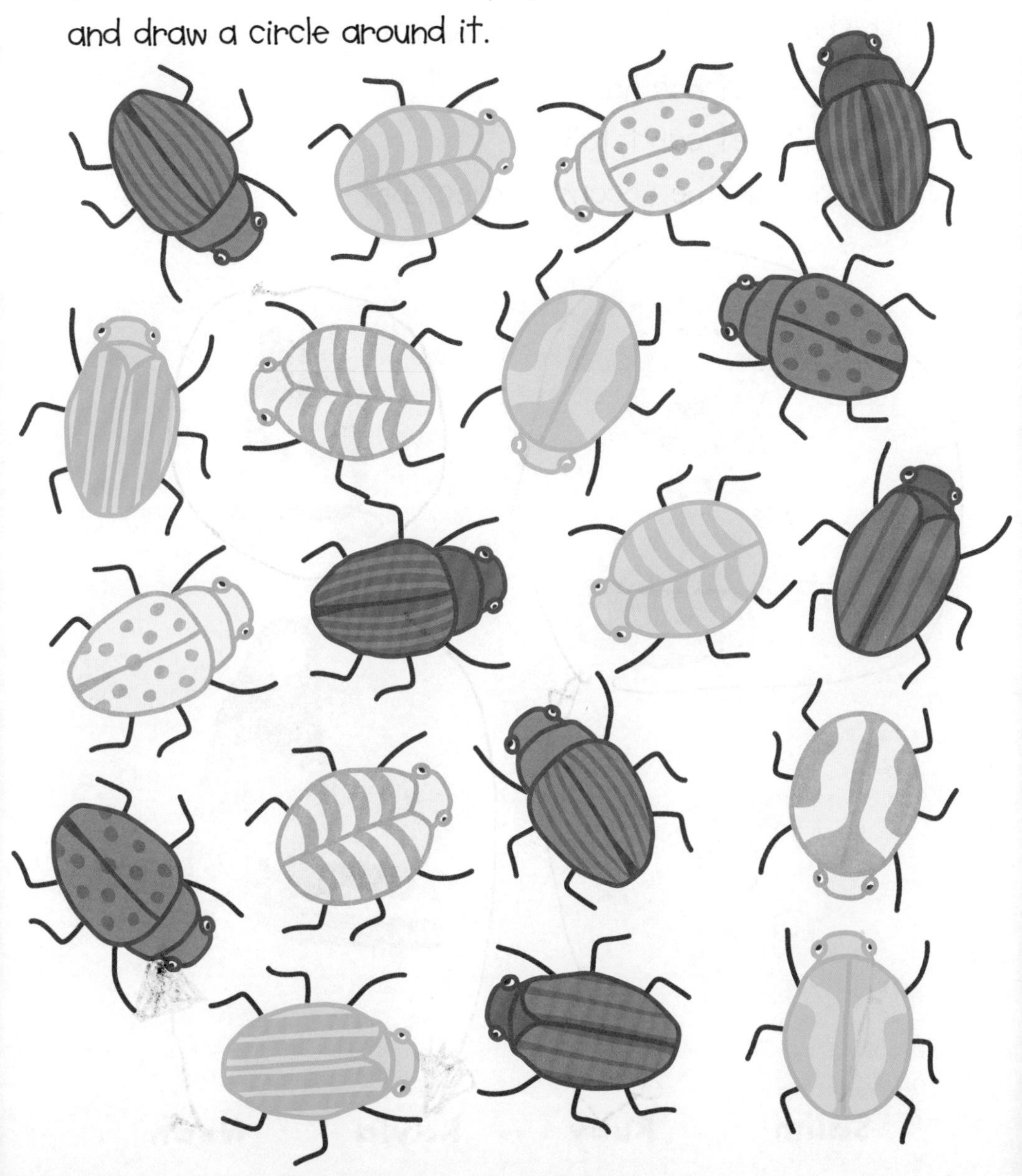

Whose pet?

Use the clues below to work out which pet belongs to which child, then draw lines to join them up.

- Ruby's pet has hair.
- Noah's pet can't talk.
- Kayla has the second-smallest pet.

Spot the starfish

All these orange starfish look the same, but one is slightly different. Can you find it?

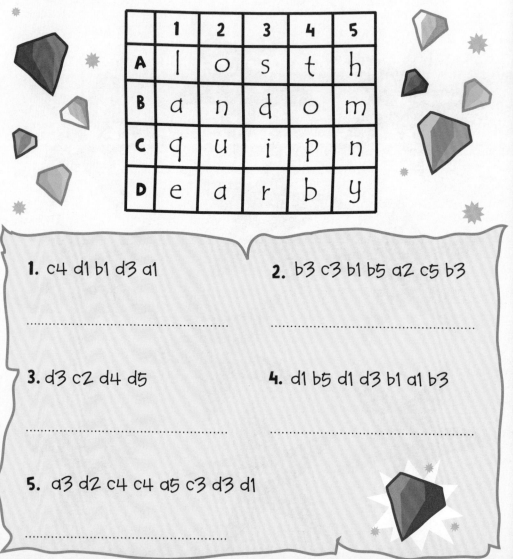

Lost jewels

Five precious gems have been stolen from an ancient temple. Use the code key grid to find out what has been lost.

	1	2	3	4	5
A	l	o	s	t	h
B	a	n	d	o	m
C	q	u	i	p	n
D	e	a	r	b	y

1. c4 d1 b1 d3 a1

....

2. b3 c3 b1 b5 a2 c5 b3

....

3. d3 c2 d4 d5

....

4. d1 b5 d1 d3 b1 a1 b3

....

5. a3 d2 c4 c4 a5 c3 d3 d1

....

Farmyard jumble

How many farm animals can you see here?

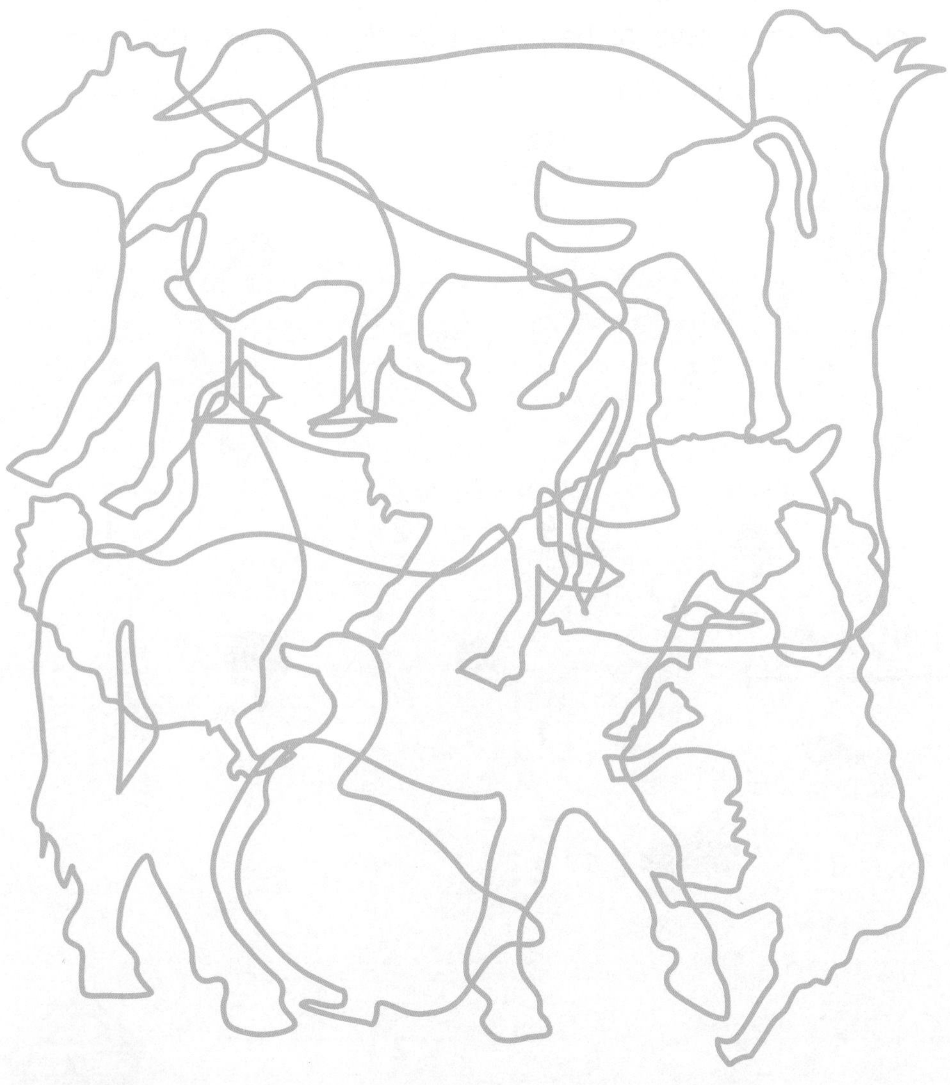

Answer:..

79

On the bus

Help the bus find its way to school, picking up passengers without becoming too overcrowded. Each stop shows the number of people to be picked up there. Draw the route the bus should take to pick up exactly 35 passengers.

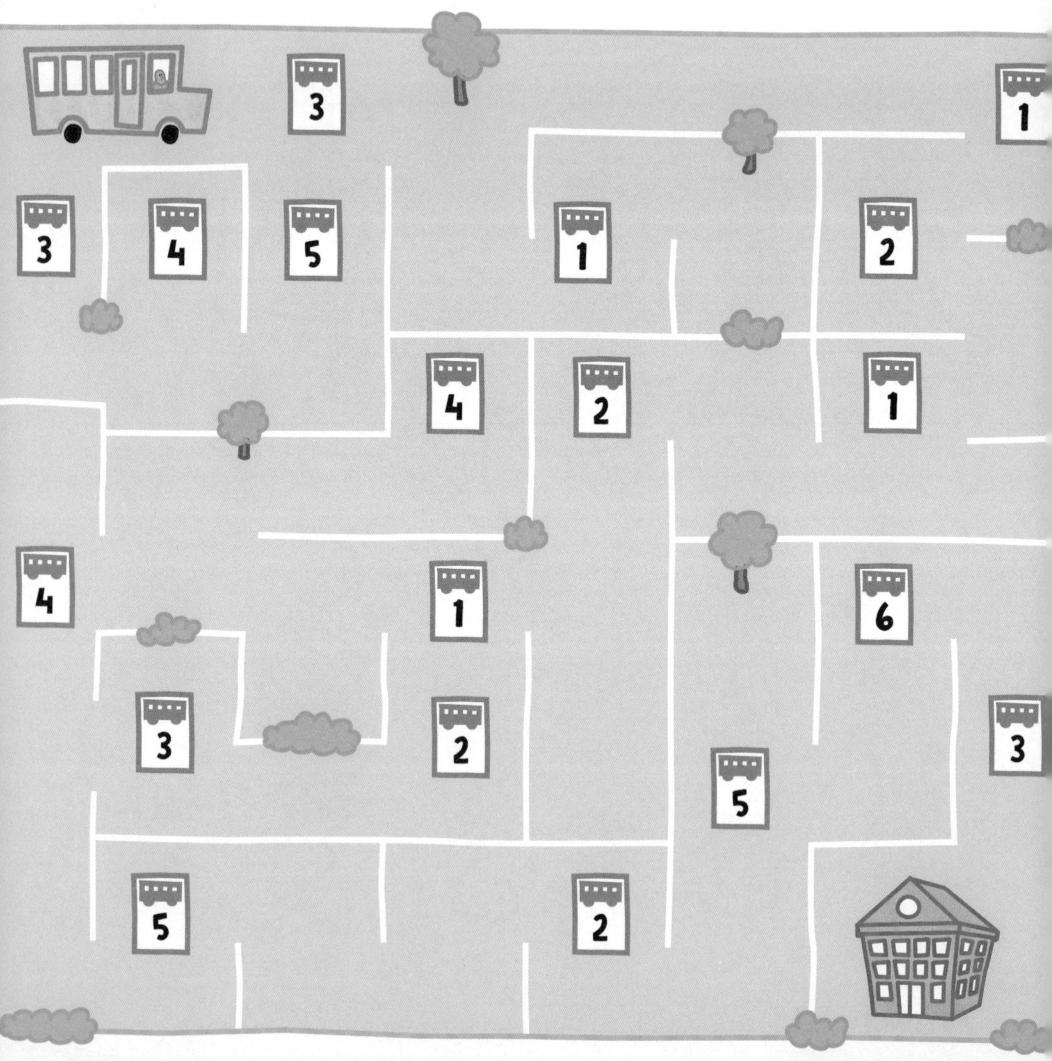

Word cross

Put a letter in the middle of each cross to make three-letter words in its arms.

1.

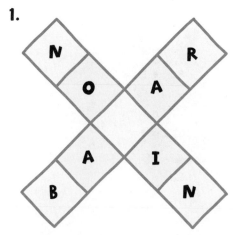

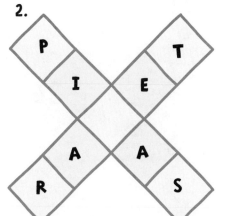

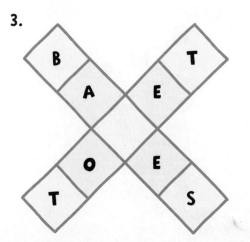

N R
O A
A I
B N

2.

P T
I E
A A
R S

3.

B T
A E
O E
T S

4.

D T
I A
I U
A D

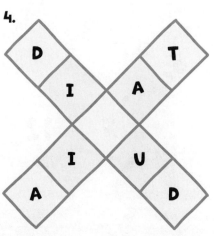

81 Number monster

This little monster eats numbers, chews them up, then spits out new numbers. Find out what the monster does to all the numbers it eats, then fill in the gaps below.

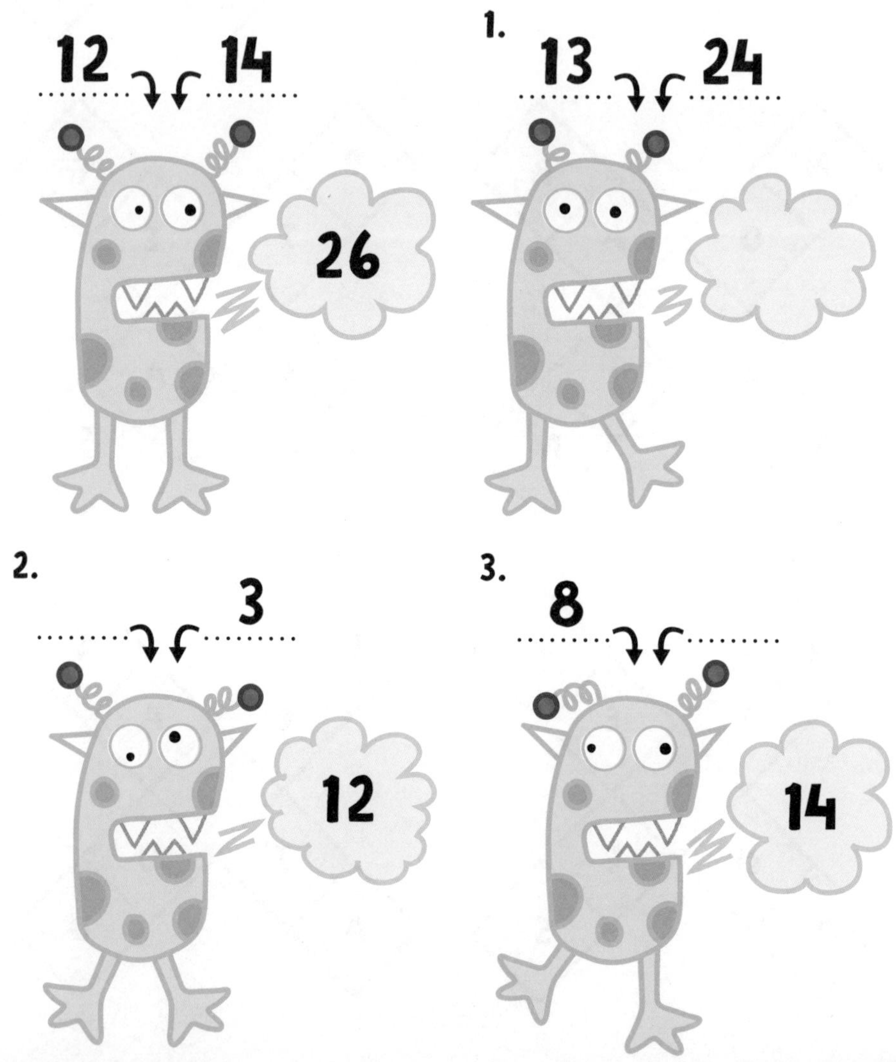

Shapes and boxes

The shapes between the boxes show you how much more or less they are worth than the next box. See if you can fill the empty boxes.

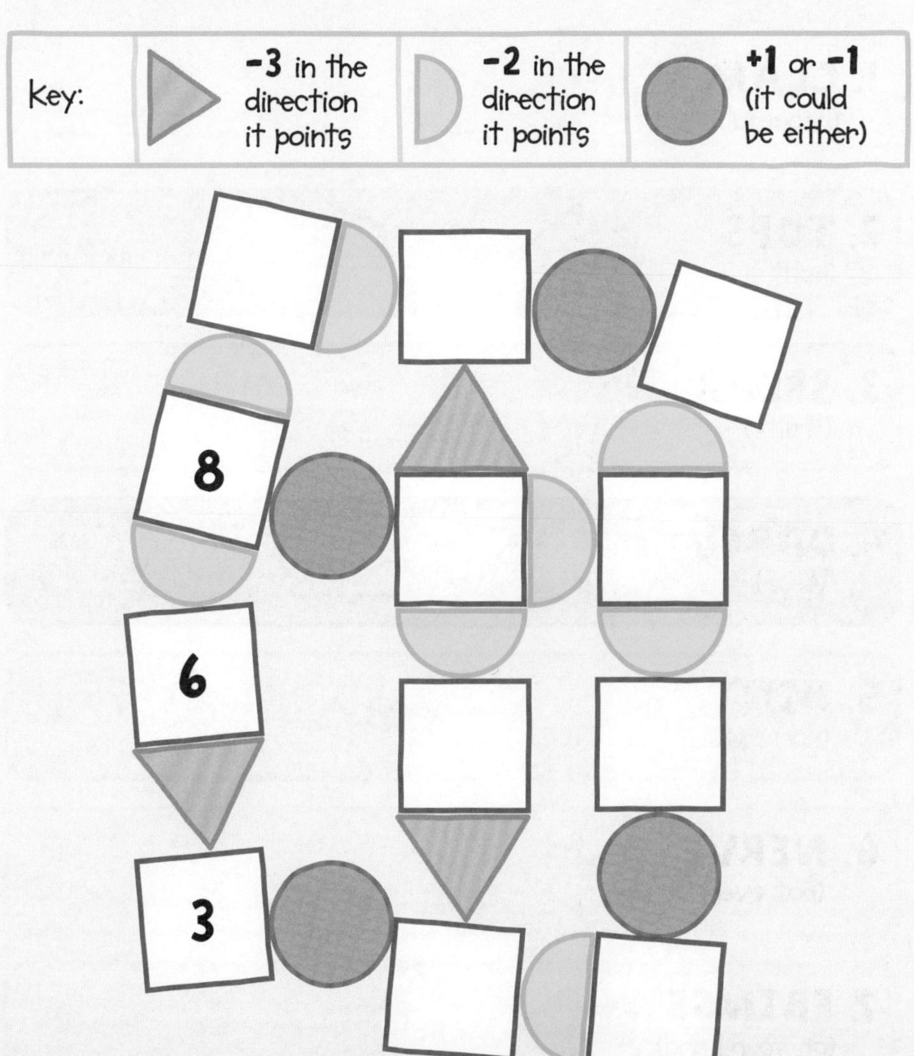

83

Lively letters

Some words can be turned into other words just by moving one letter, for example, shore → horse. Use the clues to help you find the new words below.

1. CLAM (peaceful) → ....

2. TOPS (halt) → ....

3. SPEAR (fruits) → ....

4. DARED (fear) → ....

5. HINT (narrow) → ....

6. NERVE (not ever) → ....

7. FRINGE (on your hand) → ....

Riddle grid

Cross out all the letters of the riddle below, in the grid, then rearrange the letters left behind to find the answer.

What belongs to you, but others use it more than you?

s	t	r	e	s	r	g
o	w	y	u	o	t	h
e	s	o	y	y	o	e
n	o	u	h	n	u	o
i	h	a	m	r	e	n
a	a	b	t	m	b	t
t	u	u	l	t	e	o

Answer: ....

Camouflage

The names of twenty trees are hidden below.
See if you can find them all.

saplingbarkelder
leafthinkinghazelforward
wardrobeweaverbirdlarchtrunk
squarechestnutechorunepopular
brownusefulbeechrummagecirclehope
rootamazingcollegecluehollynext
lessaspenspoonlurchfoggynapkinout
sillyfussywillowarehandstandoldertrue
boggleoakthenbecausesoundsowldriverwalnutcloudy
pressboomuncletrucewrapperhorseelbow
twinklepoplarpencilmaskthankyou
treasuresteeringashfishwheelfertile
twigelmusefulsquareforget
sprucereallystrangebranch
paniccypressstanddig
oldlimebold
growsmaple
bircheach
beamyewewe
piepipepine

What's the link?

Find a word that can be added to the end of one word and the beginning of the next. For example:

	POLICE	DOG	BISCUIT
1.	FLAP	....	POT
2.	HOBBY	....	SHOE
3.	WOOD	....	SHOP
4.	LEAP	....	SPAWN
5.	DOUBLE	....	EYED
6.	PEPPER	....	FLAKE
7.	GREEN	....	FLY

Odd ones out

Draw a circle around the odd one out in each group.

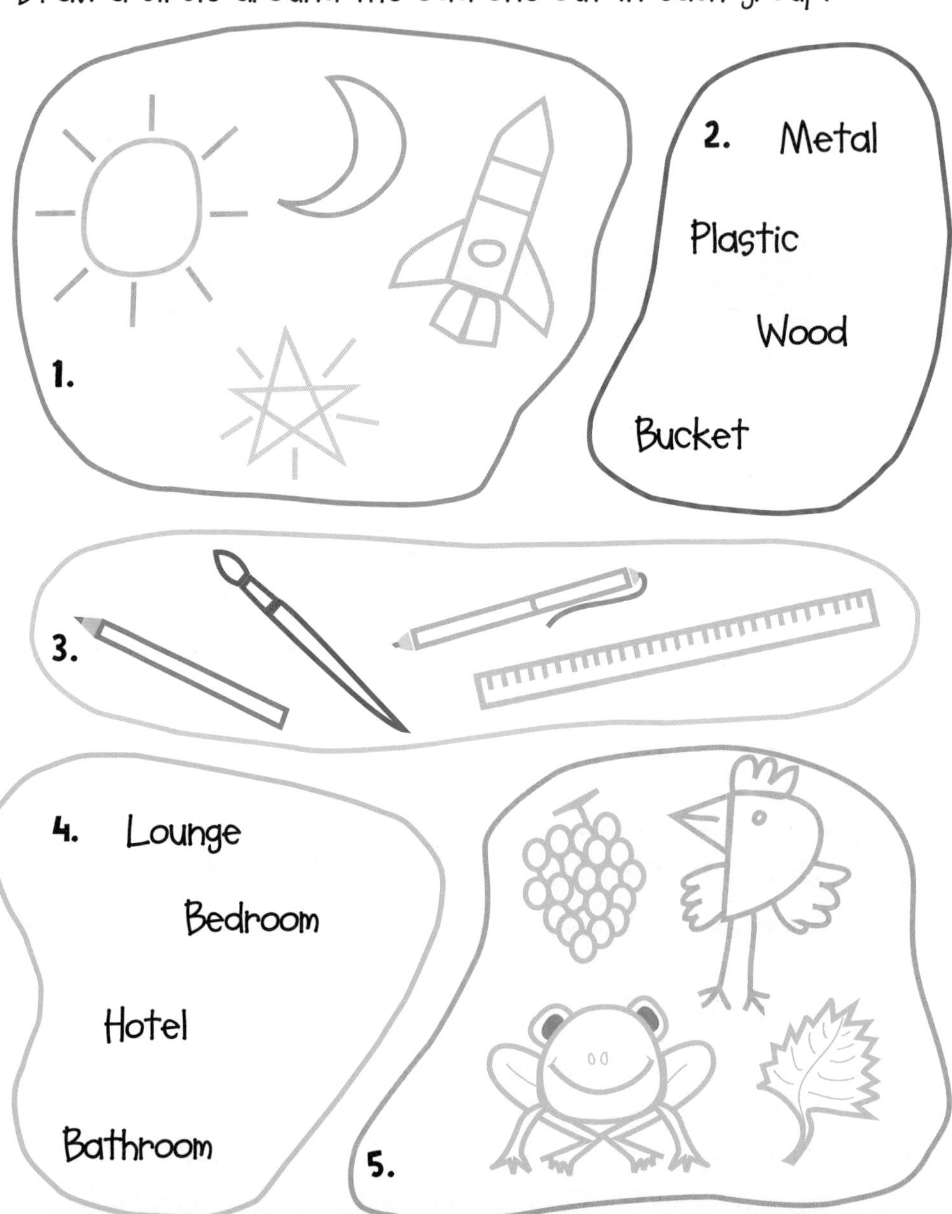

Double vision

Copy the drawings across into the blank spaces to see two complete pictures of an alien in a space rocket.

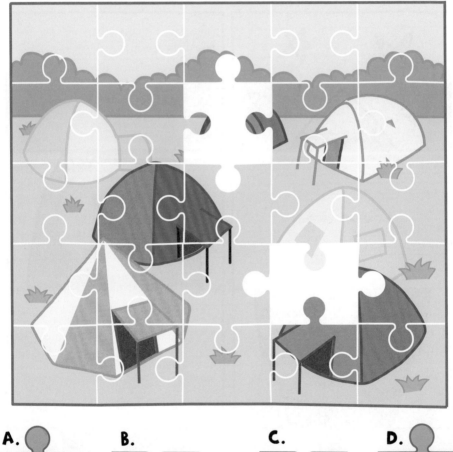

Campsite jigsaw

Circle the two pieces that are missing from this jigsaw.

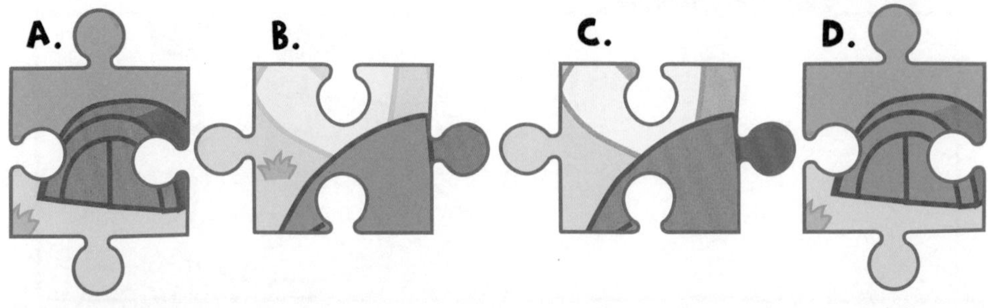

Dotty dominoes

All the dominoes but one in each row follow a pattern. Add the missing dots to make the pattern right.

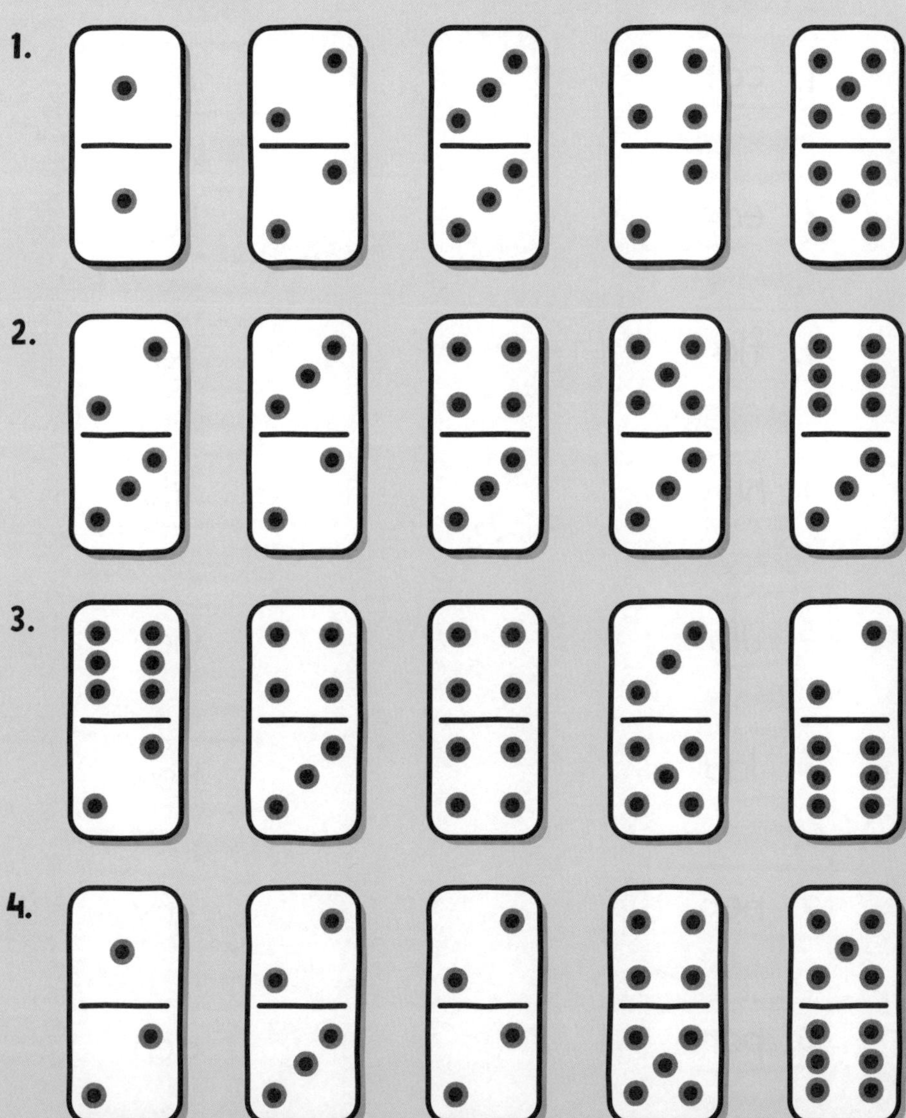

Shredded words

The words below have been broken in two. Find their missing endings, then draw a line to join them.

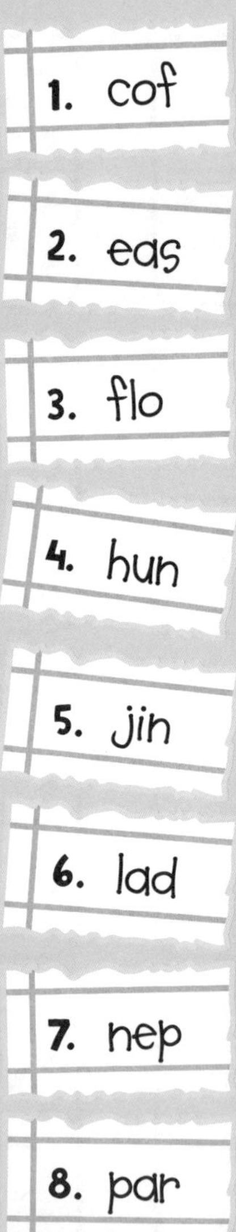

gle

fee

rot

ily

wer

hew

gry

der

Boat race

Use the clues below to work out the positions of the boats in the race, then draw lines to join them up.

- Skylark didn't come last.
- No boat named after a bird came first.
- Tulip came between boats named after birds.

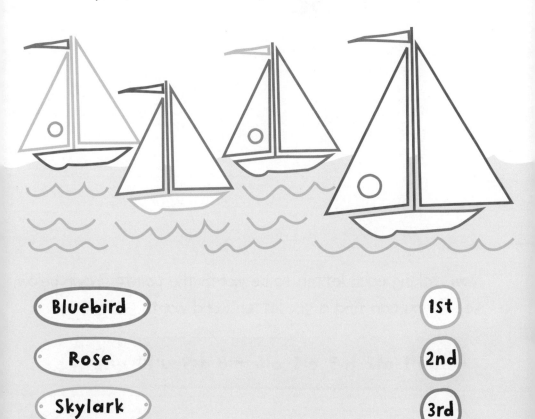

Bluebird	**1st**
Rose	**2nd**
Skylark	**3rd**
Tulip	**4th**

Word count

Use any of these letters to make as many words as you can. You can use each letter only once.

a h o u

n g i e t

....

....

....

....

Now, taking each letter to be worth the points shown below, see if you can find a six-letter word worth 50 points.

i:1 a:2 h:3 e:5 o:6 n:8 t:9 u:10 g:12

For example, 'night' would be worth 8+1+12+3+9=33 points.

Answer: .... (Clue: in your mouth)

Hopping frog

Every time Freddy the Frog lands on a lily pad, he stops and eats two flies. How many flies has he eaten by the time he reaches the:

- flower? ....
- dragonfly? ....
- snail? ....
- duckling? ....

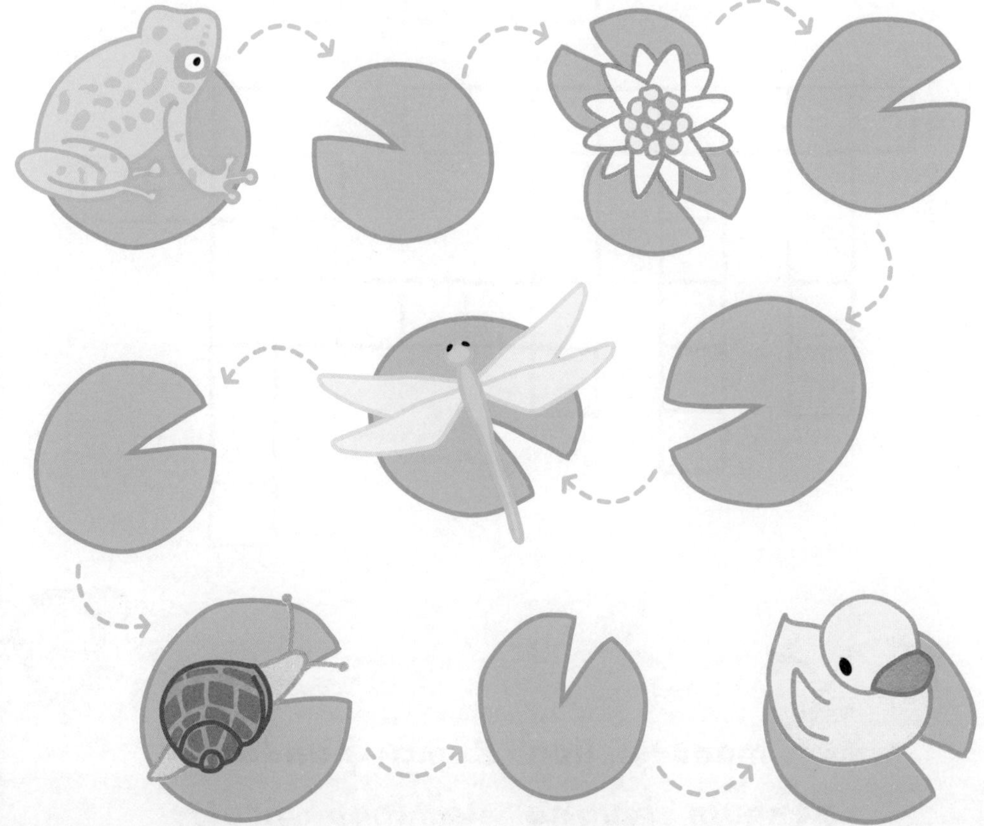

Zoo crisscross

Fit the names of the zoo animals below into the squares.

monkey lion llama panda

penguin iguana flamingo giraffe

Giant turtle

Make a larger copy of the turtle in the bigger grid below.

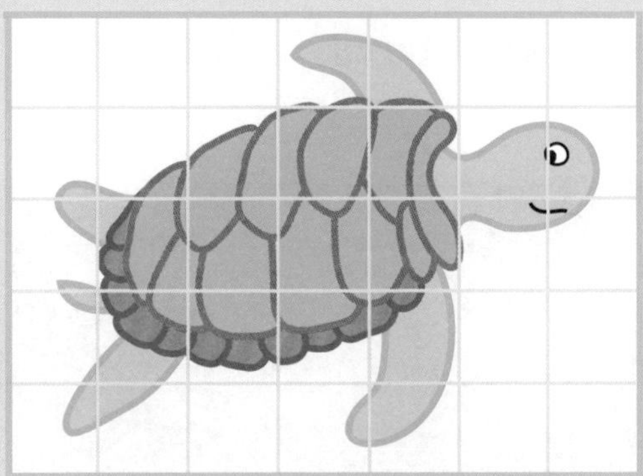

Cross-sum

Place numbers in the grid so that each row and column adds up to the total shown in the arrow. Each number in a row or column must be different.

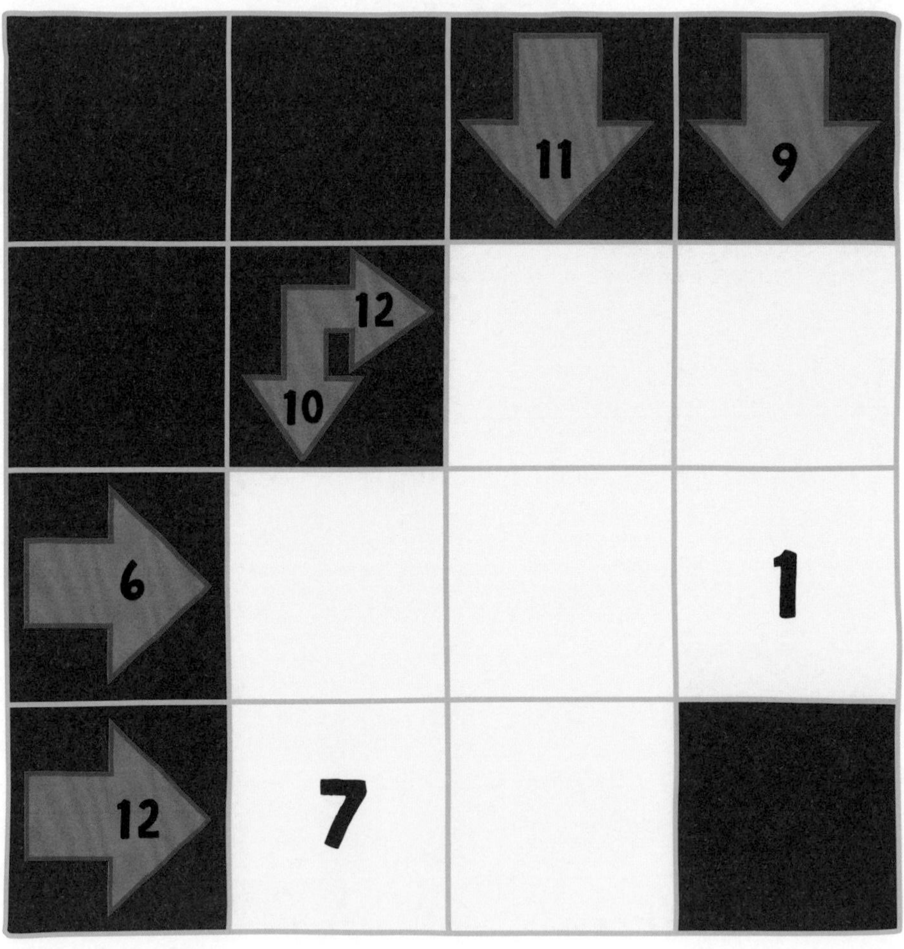

Jumbled jokes

Draw lines to join the questions to the right answers and make these jokes funny (or awful) again.

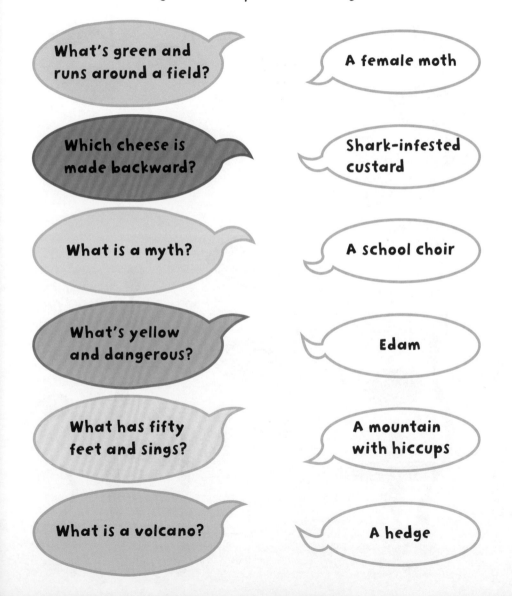

What's green and runs around a field?

A female moth

Which cheese is made backward?

Shark-infested custard

What is a myth?

A school choir

What's yellow and dangerous?

Edam

What has fifty feet and sings?

A mountain with hiccups

What is a volcano?

A hedge

Identical fins

Only two of these fish are exactly the same.
See if you can find them.

Find the city

Read the descriptions and fill in the missing letters to make words that match them. Then join up the new letters to make the name of a big city in California, USA.

1. Mad, crazy in..........ne
2. Moveable amusement park fu..........air
3. Villain of the seas pi ....te
4. Wooden writing tool pe..........il
5. Sounds no..........es
6. Small American mammal with dark 'mask' rac..........on

Answer: ....

Name game

Arrange the six girls' names in the grid below so that the yellow squares spell out a boy's name.

J					
		S			
					H

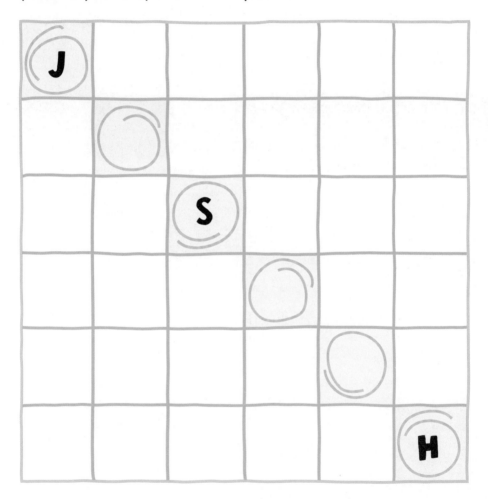

ANGELA **JULIET** **HANNAH**

FELIPA **CASSIE** **SOPHIE**

Giant beanstalk

Climb the giant beanstalk by filling in the missing numbers in each sequence.

Arctic animals

See if you can fit these animals from the far north into the grid.

arctic fox
killer whale
polar bear
snowy owl
caribou
narwhal
ermine
walrus

On target

Score this archery contest, and find the winner.

Scores:

Rufus: ....

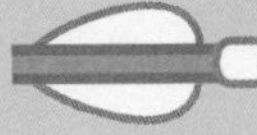

Eva: ....

Chris: ....

Violet: ....

105

Ferris wheel

How many people will have passed the point where the top red gondola is now (including those inside it) in the time it takes it to reach the position of the lower red gondola?

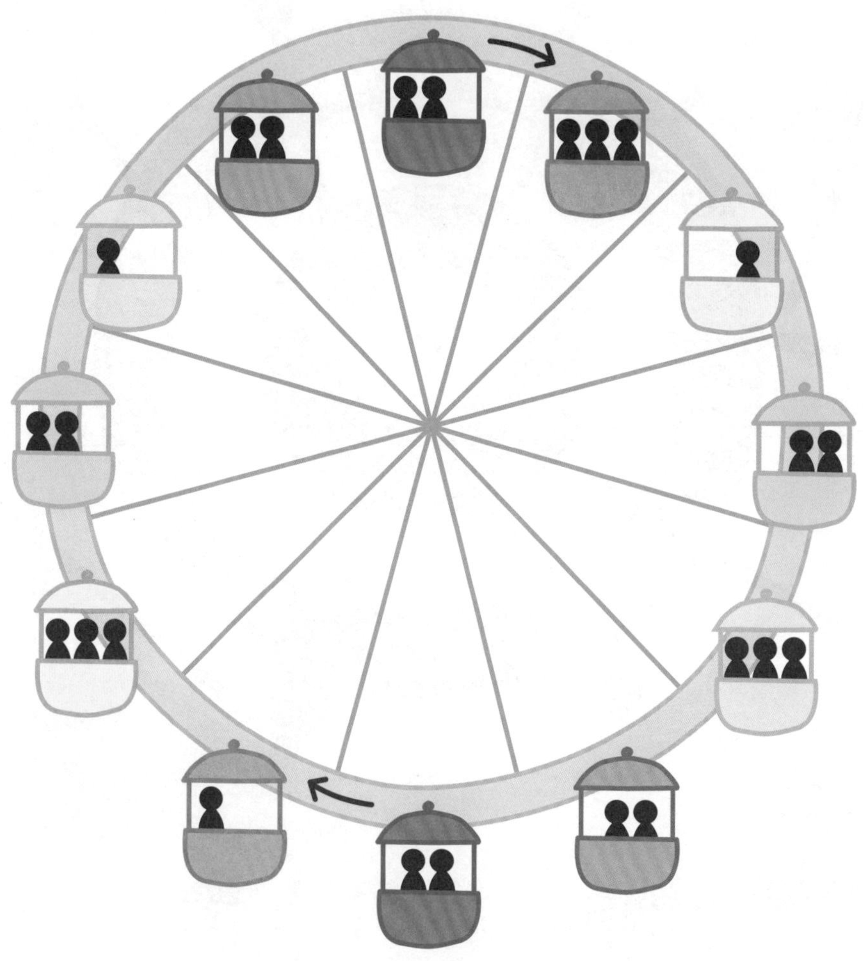

Answer:...

Spelling secrets

You might think that the writer of this letter can't spell, but in fact she is a spy. The wrong or extra letters can be joined up to spell out a secret message.

Deer Mother,

Thanxyou for the topp you sent mee. It was very nicce oft you. I loave the desigm. Whan cann I visiit? Is Nonday ok? I'll bbring those glovels you left aat my placce. Kan you remindd me, oor I'm bounnd too forgett? Perfaps wee caan go forr a thrip to the citey? I'd liike to sees it agaan. I hafe many memorries of iits brighte lights. See you soonn!

Love andd kisses

Paula xxx

Secret message:

Odd gnome out

Which gnome is different from the rest?

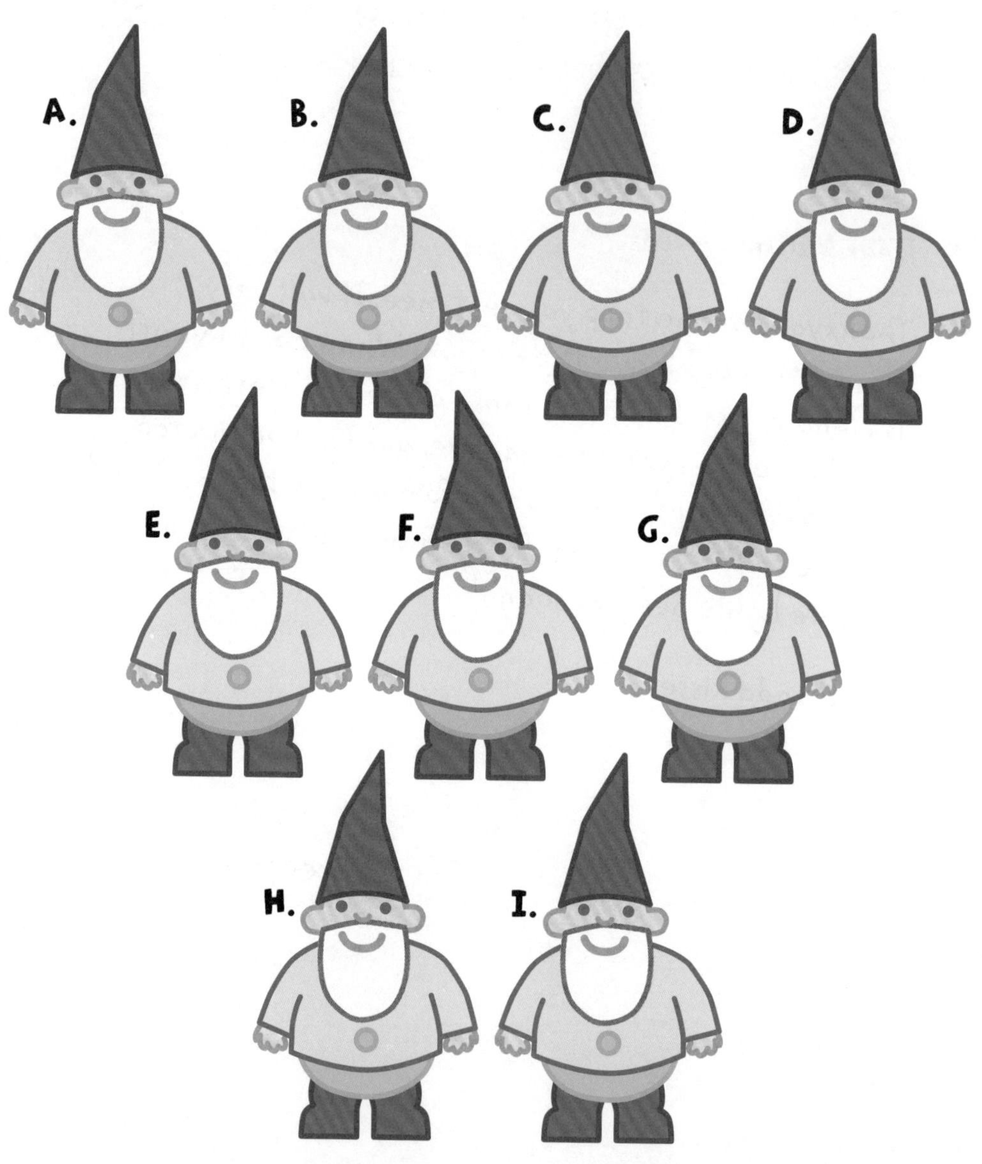

Doorsteps

The house number has fallen off this door. To find it, write the missing numbers on the blank steps. Each number is the sum of the two directly underneath it. The sum of the two numbers on the top step is the missing house number. Write it on the door.

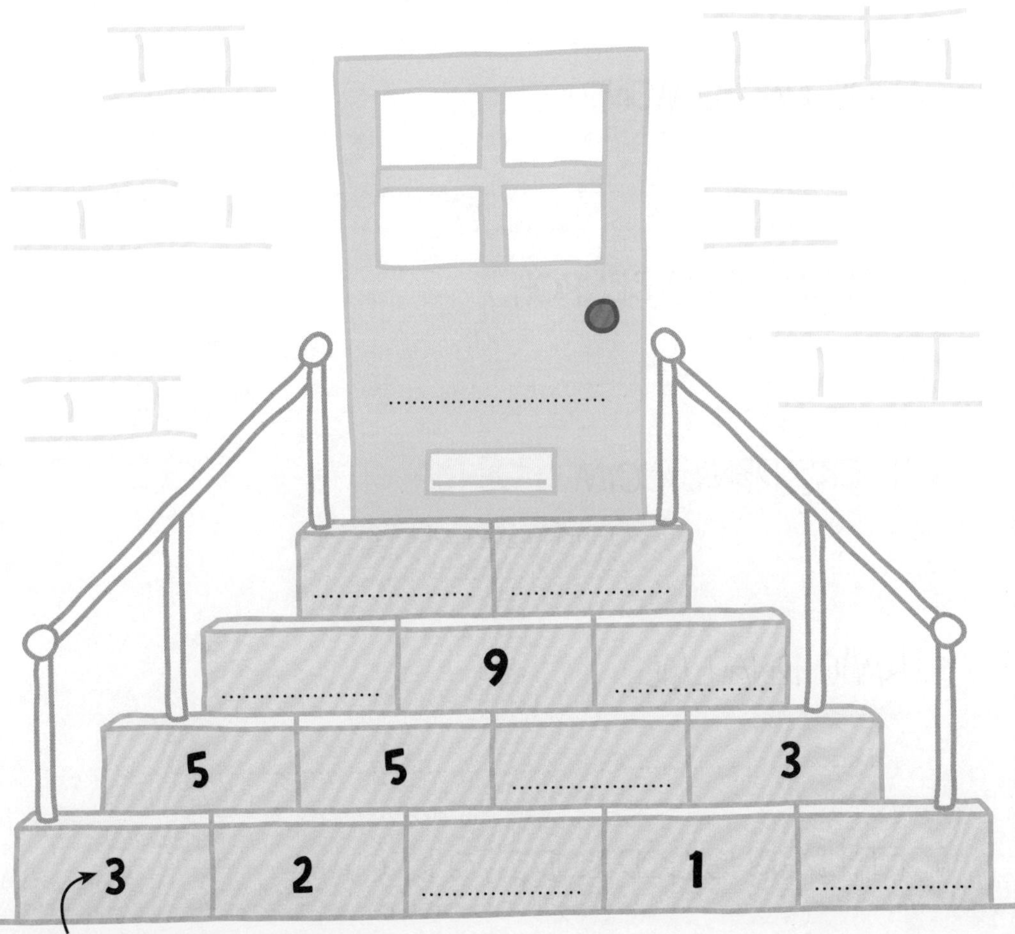

109 Nursery rhyme mix-up

See if you can unscramble the mixed-up names of the nursery rhyme characters below.

1. MYTHUP TYMPUD

....

2. DOL CADALMOND

....

3. TELLIT AKCJ RENROH

....

4. THERE DBNIL ECIM

....

5. KAJC DNA LIJL

....

6. ETH DRANG LOD KUDE FO KROY

....

Desert crisscross

See if you can fit these desert animals into the grid.

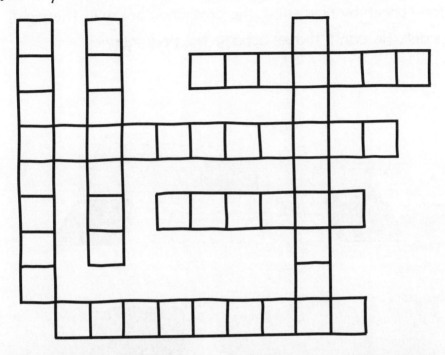

scorpion **meerkat** **fennec fox** **armadillo**
rattlesnake **vulture** **gerbil**

Robot power

Program the robot to move onto the blue square in the far corner by numbering the commands below in the right order. He can't travel across the red squares.

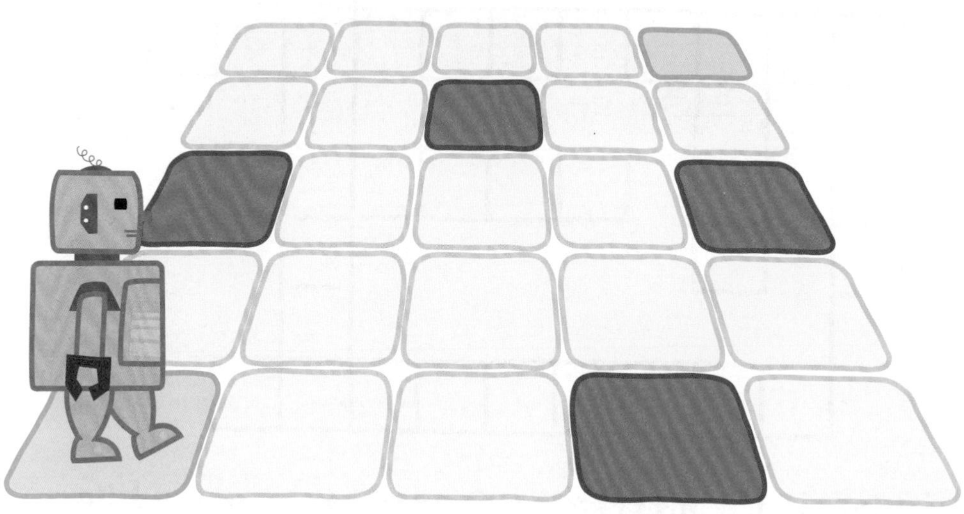

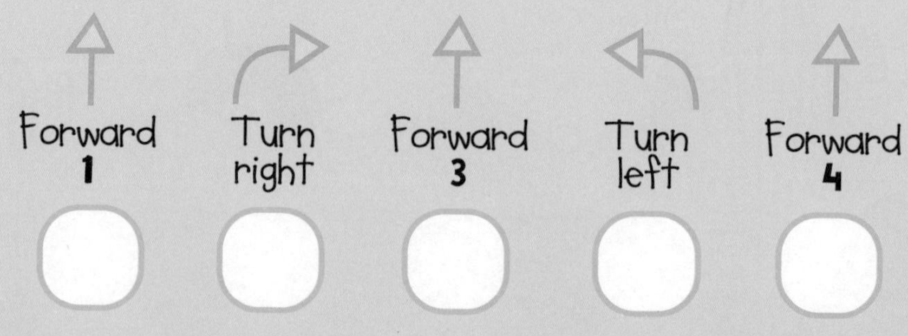

Thumbprint maze

Find your way from A to B through the thumbprint.

Island in the sun

Cross out all the types of shapes listed at the bottom of the page, then write out the letters on the remaining shapes to find the name of an island in the Caribbean Sea.

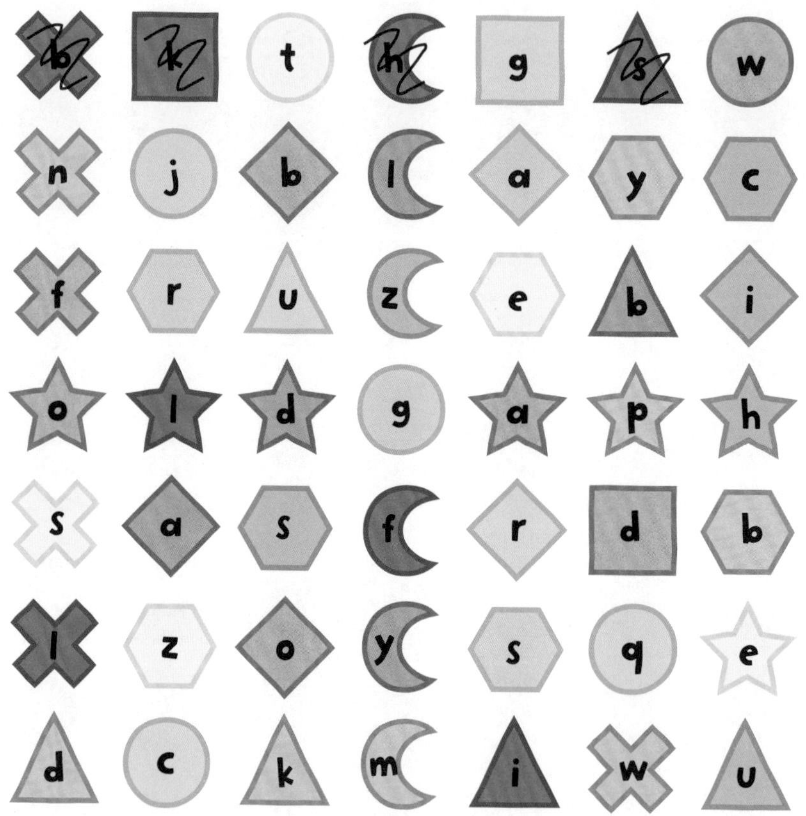

Red shapes　Stars　Green shapes　Moons　Crosses

Circles　Yellow shapes　Pink shapes

....

Capital quiz

See how many of these capital cities you can match to their countries. Write them on the labels.

Russia France China Japan

Australia United Kingdom United States

115

Beach pairs

These beach towels come in pairs. The towels in each pair have the same pattern as each other. Circle the towel that isn't part of a pair.

Spotted bugs

Look at the spotted bugs for a minute, then cover them and try to draw the right number of spots on the bugs below.

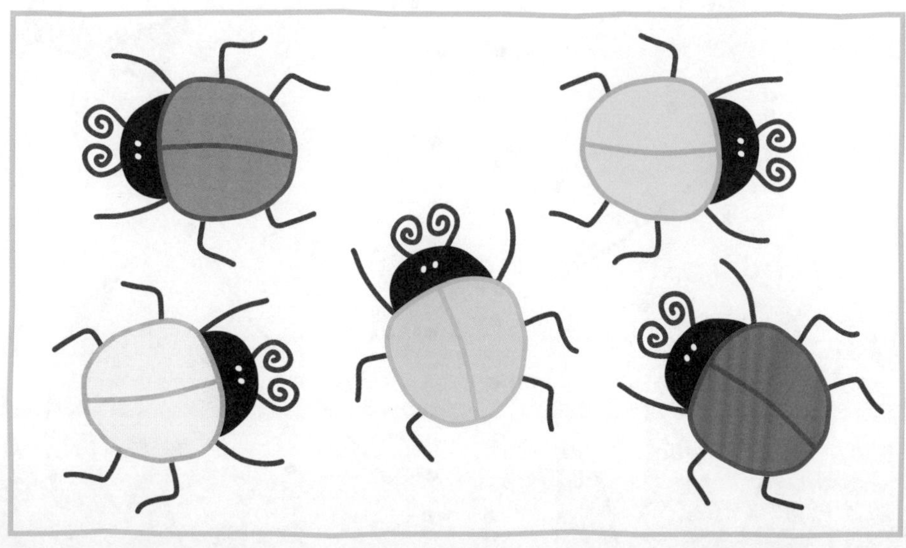

In the garden

Join the dots in order to see what's growing in the garden.

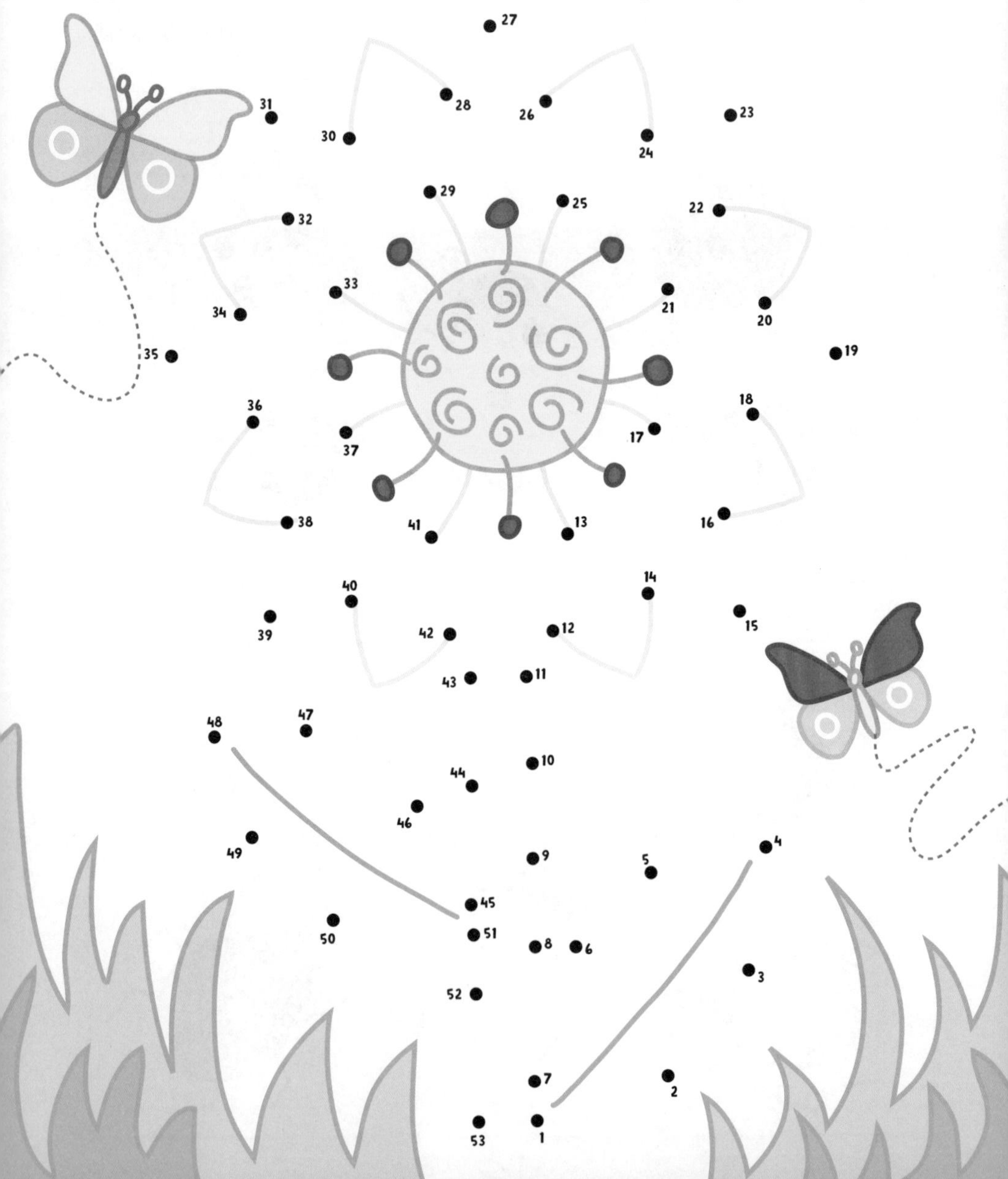

Cross-sum

Place numbers in the grid so that each row and column adds up to the total shown by the arrow. Each number in a row or column must be different.

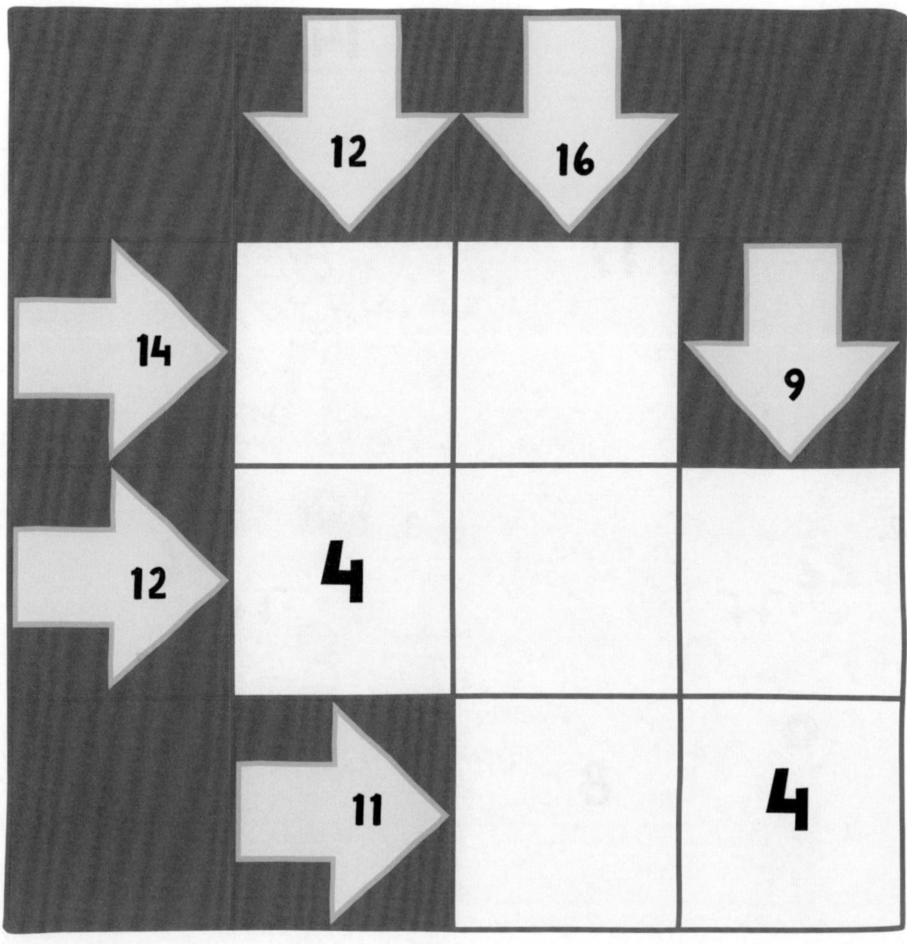

Number monster

This little monster eats numbers, chews them up, then spits out new numbers. Find out what the monster does to all the numbers it eats, then fill in the gaps below.

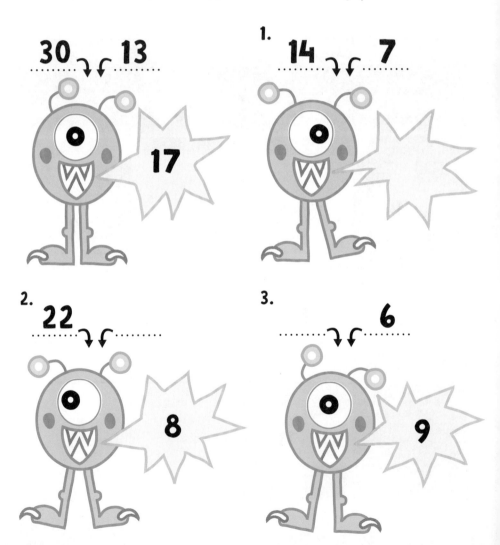

30 .... 13 ....

17

1\. 14 .... 7 ....

2\. 22 ....

8

3\. .... 6 ....

9

Number cross

1. Try to fit the number names into the squares below.

one	**two**	**three**	**four**	**five**	**six**
seven	**eight**	**nine**	**ten**	**eleven**	**twelve**

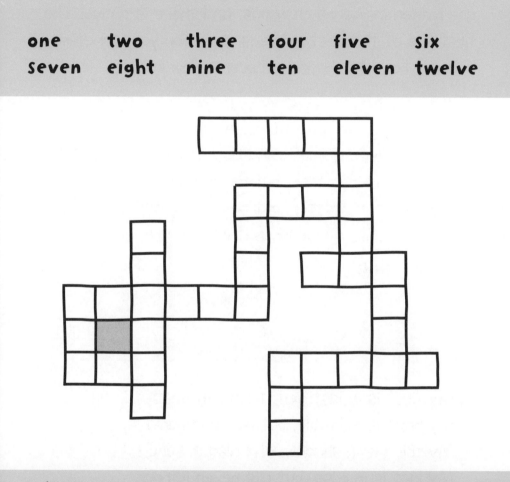

2. Bonus question: which number is equal to the number of letters in its name?

Answer: ....

121

What am I?

In the riddles below, the letters that spell the answers are hidden inside other words, and there is a clue. The first line of the first riddle is given for you; sometimes you may have to choose between a few letters.

1. My first is in food, but it isn't in fool
My next is in wooden, and also in tool
My third is in coffee, but never in juice
My last is in rooster, but never in goose
My whole fills a hole when it isn't in use

~~f~~~~o~~~~o~~d ~~f~~~~o~~~~o~~~~l~~

....

....

2. My first is in last, but it isn't in first
My next is in bubble, but never in burst
My third is in shadow, and also in sure
My last is in rose, but it's never in roar
Before you had me I am sure you had more

....

....

Optical illusions

Study the images below closely, then try to answer the questions.

1. Is one of these circles bigger than the other?

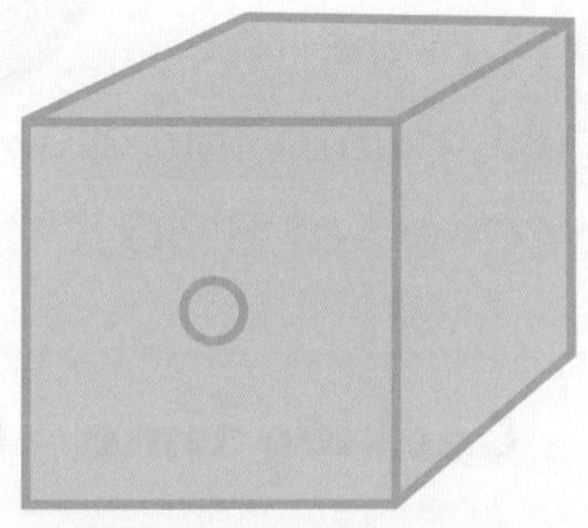

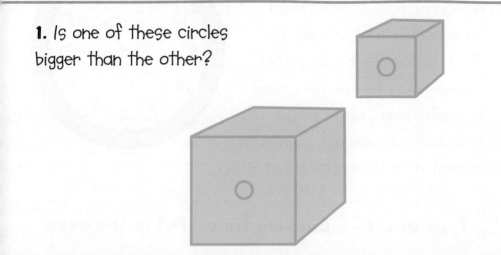

2. Are the lines between the little squares straight or curved?

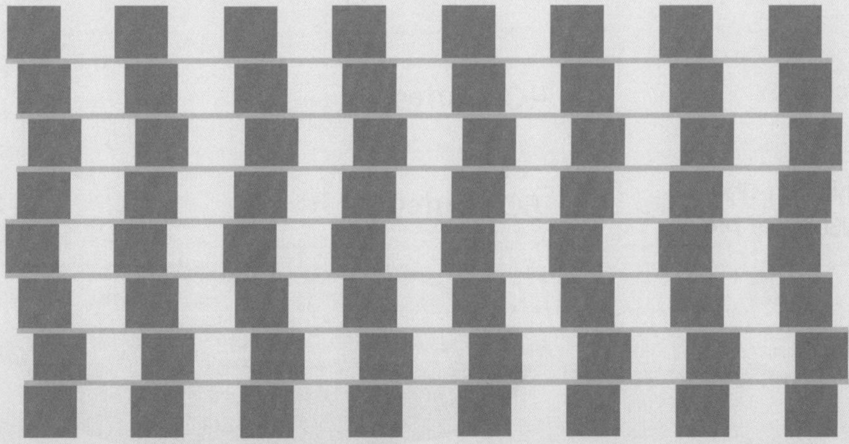

123 Perfect pies

At the Perfect Pie restaurant, the chef has an order for four different pies that all need to be ready at the same time. Take a look at the chart below to see how long the pies need to cook. Then, write in the time that each one should go into the oven if it is to be served at 8:30.

Type of pie	Cooking time	Put in the oven
Cheese and leek pie	25 minutes	
Vegetable pie	35 minutes	
Fish pie	40 minutes	
Chicken and mushroom pie	50 minutes	

Dotty dominoes

All the dominoes but one in each row follow a pattern.
Blot out the extra dots to make the pattern right.

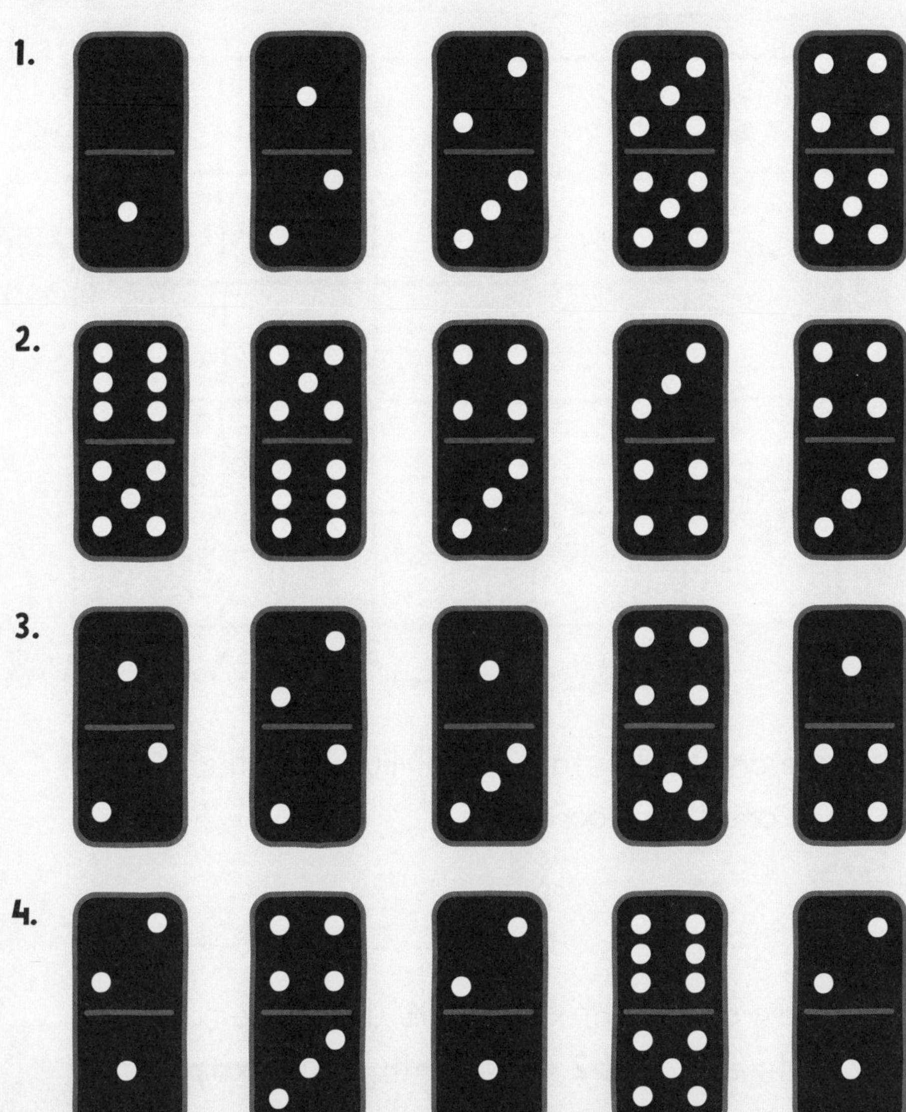

125 Buried treasure

A brave explorer has set up a camp in the desert at coordinates (**2**, **1**) on the map below.

1. There are three statues half-buried in the desert. What are their coordinates?

 ...., ...

 ...., ...

 ...., ...

2. There's an ancient king's tomb under the sand, **2** units east and **2** units north of the camp. Mark its position with an X.

Crossword

ACROSS

1. piece
2. wild, dog-like animal
5. prize
7. very fast spotted big cat
10. tale
11. 12 months
12. noise made by 2 across

DOWN

1. what peas grow in
3. flame
4. King Arthur's castle
5. remains of a fire
6. journal
8. very small
9. female child

127

Weighing in

From the readings shown on the weighing scales, can you find out the weight, in strawberries, of one...

...apple?

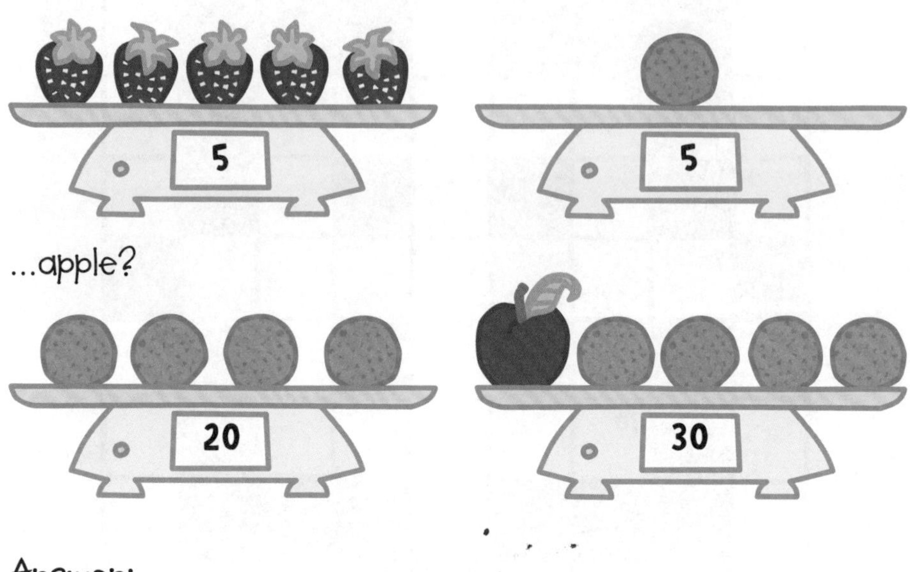

Answer:...

...watermelon?

Answer:...

Funny faces

Find the sequence, then draw the missing features on the blank face.

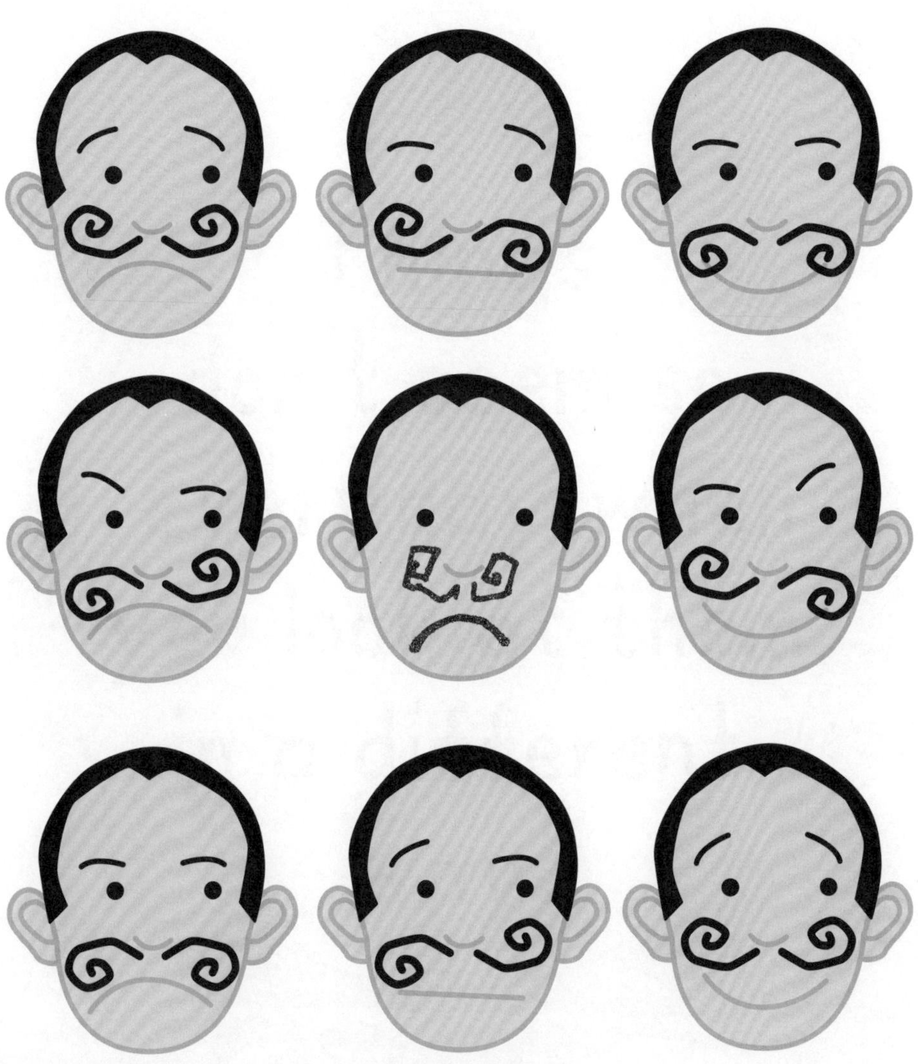

129

Mirror message

Try to read this message. If you can't, try looking at it in a mirror.

Things don't seem so everyday when you look at them in a different way.

Sounds the same

Find words in the grid that sound just like the words at the bottom, but are spelled differently. They may be written in any direction.

For example: 'fined' — look for 'find'

t	o	n	e	r	e	h	r
i	h	h	w	u	o	u	h
e	r	o	m	o	u	t	a
r	r	l	h	f	r	h	w
t	o	e	t	i	s	g	r
e	g	e	g	n	f	i	o
r	g	h	n	d	a	n	u
e	t	r	o	p	f	r	e

fined	**heal**	**hours**	**won**
for	**hear**	**knight**	**pear**
groan	**whole**	**moor**	**write**

Train parts

Circle the group of parts that can be put together to make up the train shown on the right.

A.

B.

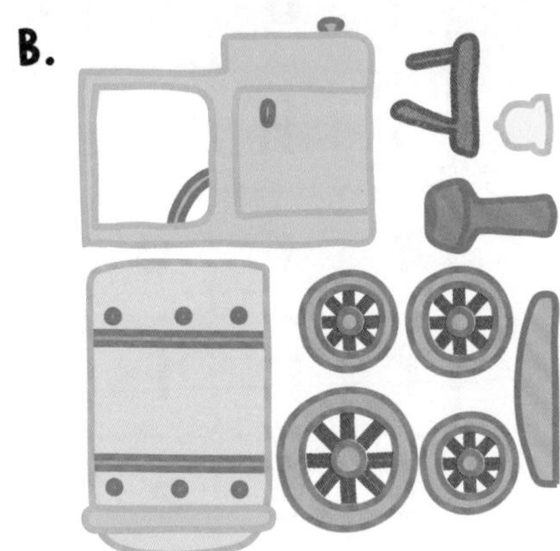

C.

D.

Beach treasure hunt

Some children have nearly reached the end of a treasure hunt on the beach. Follow the final clue to help them find the beach hut where the treasure is hidden.

The beach hut where the treasure is hidden is two places to the left of a hut whose door matches its roof. Its front wall does not have every other plank painted white, and its number isn't even.

Answer: ....

Shell search

In the picture below, draw around the group of shells that matches the group shown on the right.

Double vision

Copy the drawings across into the blank spaces to see two complete pictures of a snake in a rainforest tree.

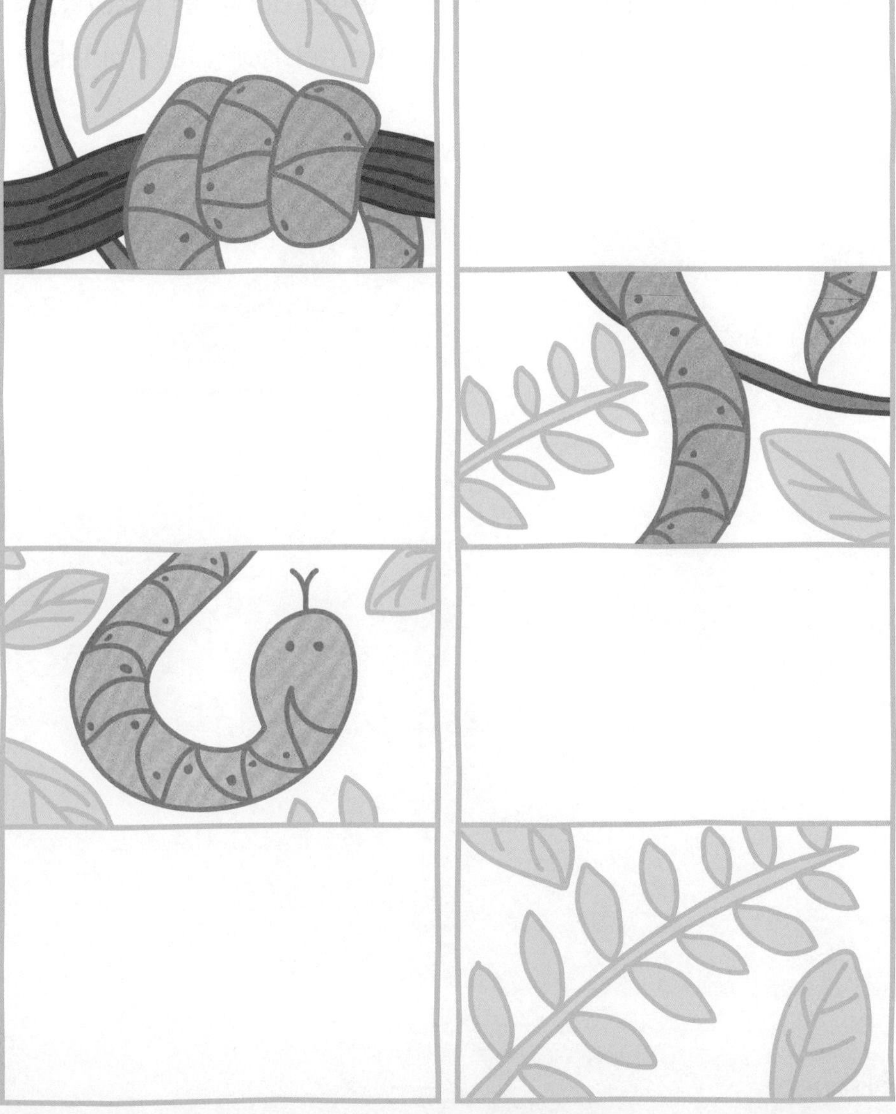

Umbrella patterns

This umbrella has eight sections.

- Draw spots on $\frac{1}{4}$ of the sections.
- Then draw stripes on $\frac{1}{3}$ of the sections left blank.
- Then draw squares on $\frac{1}{2}$ of the sections left blank.

How many sections are left without a pattern?

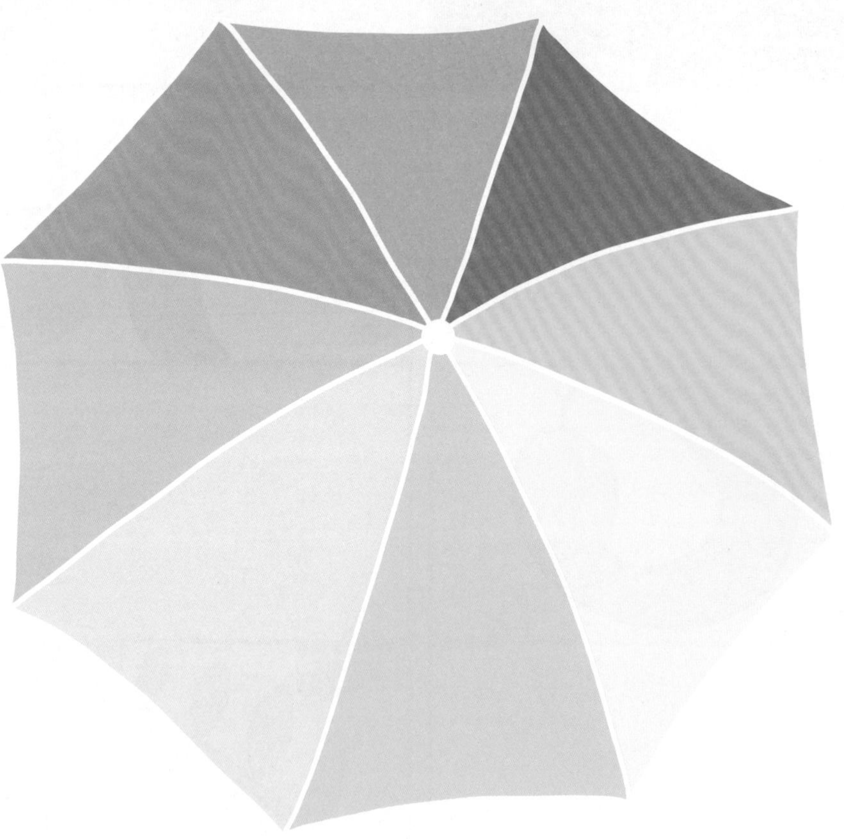

Answer:..

Sneaky letters

Help Milo the mouse sneak past the sleeping cat without waking it, by marking a path made only of letters that are silent in the word in which they appear in the grid.

W	I	S	H	L	A	M	B	S	T	O	O	L
T	O	P	C	O	U	L	D	B	R	E	W	S
N	I	C	E	A	N	S	W	E	R	S	U	N
F	L	O	W	E	R	H	O	N	E	S	T	Y
I	T	C	R	U	M	B	R	I	V	E	R	S
B	R	A	V	E	K	N	I	G	H	T	M	E
N	O	S	E	W	R	I	T	E	C	A	R	D
T	U	B	E	G	N	O	M	E	A	R	M	Y
O	F	M	U	S	C	L	E	T	H	I	N	K

Same meaning

Not all of the words in these word pairs mean the same thing. Mark them ✓ if they do or ✗ if they do not.

1.	Rush → Hurry	
2.	Dog → Animal	
3.	Anger → Rage	
4.	Alter → Change	
5.	Hold → Touch	
6.	Cheerful → Happy	
7.	Bright → Dull	
8.	Shout → Sing	

Cupcake numbers

Maisie made 12 cupcakes and numbered them. She put a cherry on every cupcake with an even number. Then, she put sprinkles on every cupcake with a number that can be divided by three. Lastly, she put a sugar star on every cupcake with a number that can be divided by four.

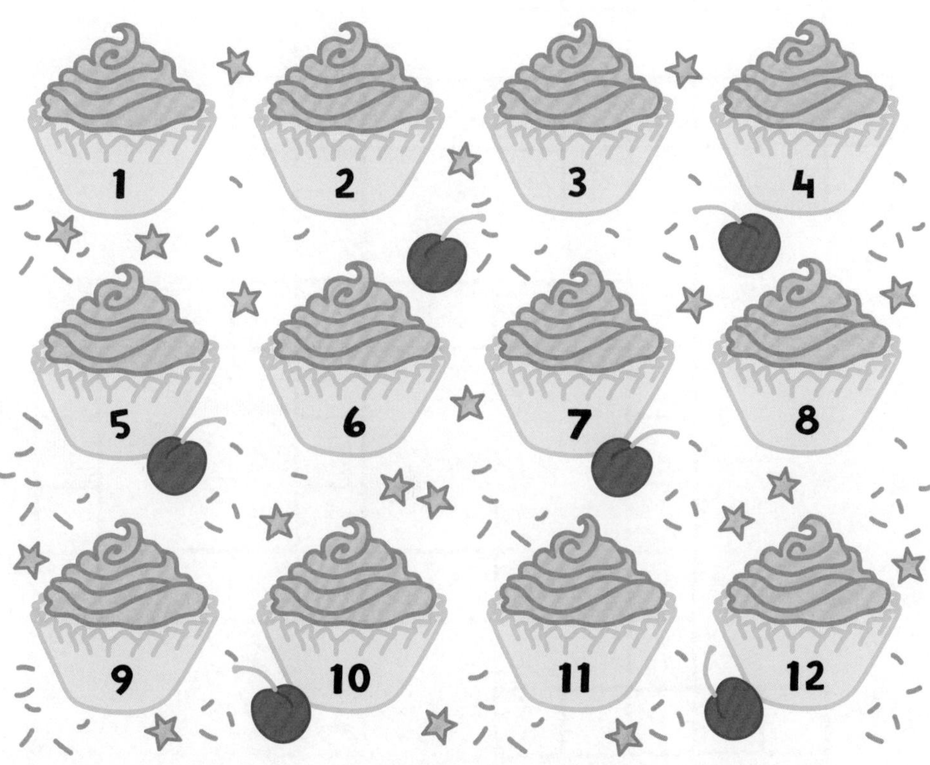

1. Which cupcakes had no decoration? ....

2. Did any get all three decorations? ....

Calendar crisscross

Try to fit the months of the year into the grid below.

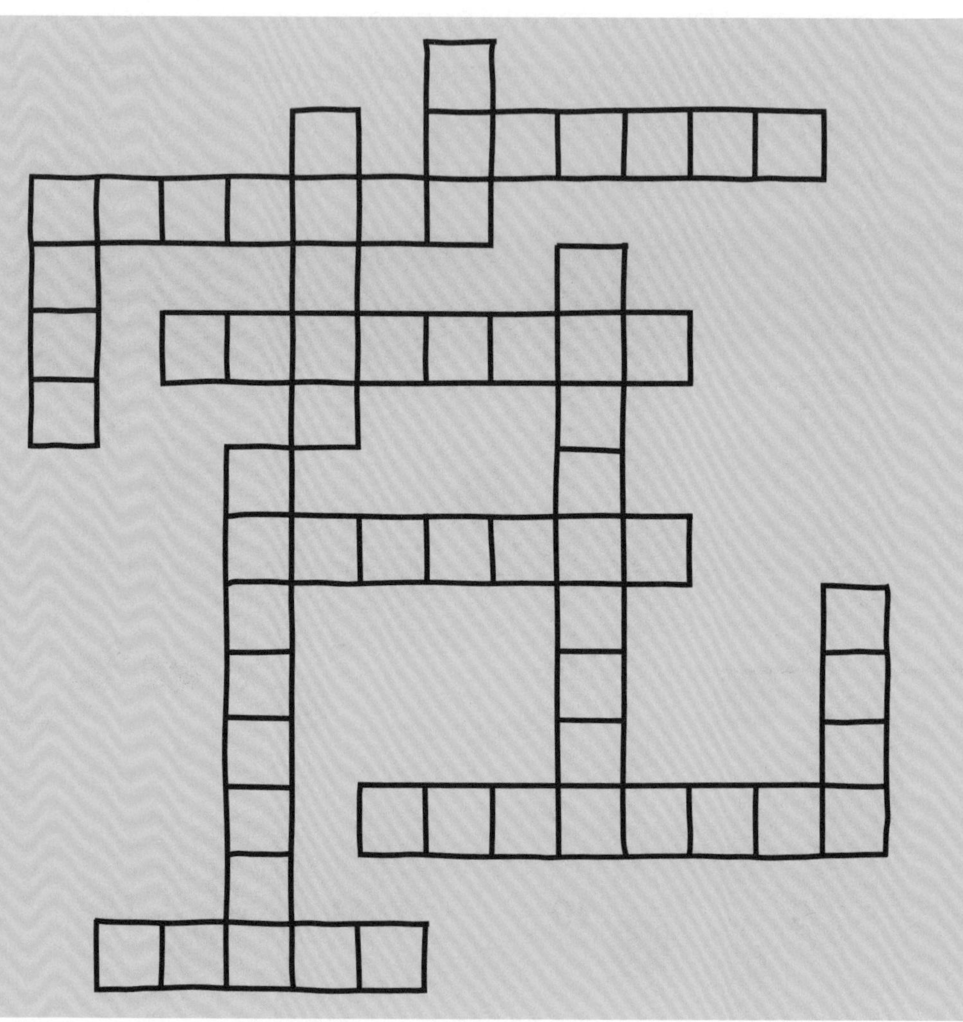

January	**April**	**July**	**October**
February	**May**	**August**	**November**
March	**June**	**September**	**December**

Alphablocks

Number the blocks at the bottom in alphabetical order, then copy their shapes into the grid to make a picture.

1.	2.	3.	4.	5.
6.	7.	8.	9.	10.
11.	12.	13.	14.	15.

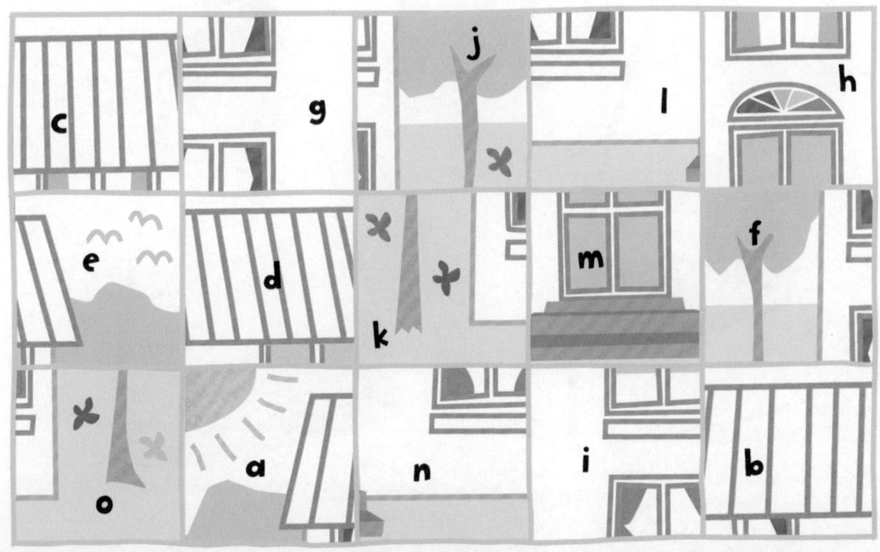

Windsurfing

Circle the two sails that are exactly the same.

Missing symbol

Try to find out the value of the symbols, and fill in the missing one. The sum of each line and column is shown.

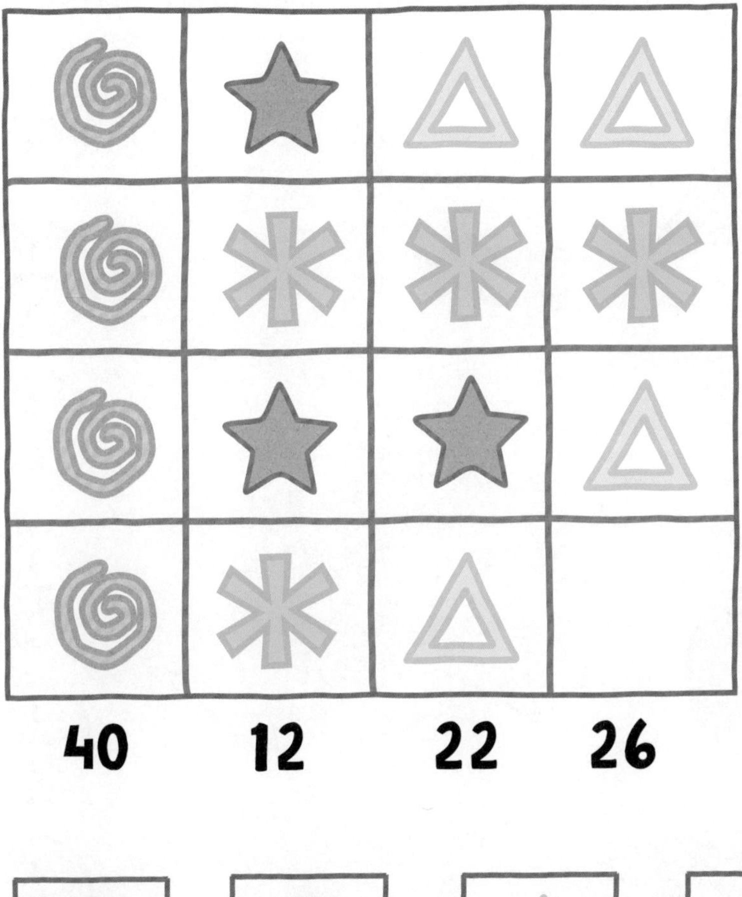

				27
				25
				20
				28
40	12	22	26	

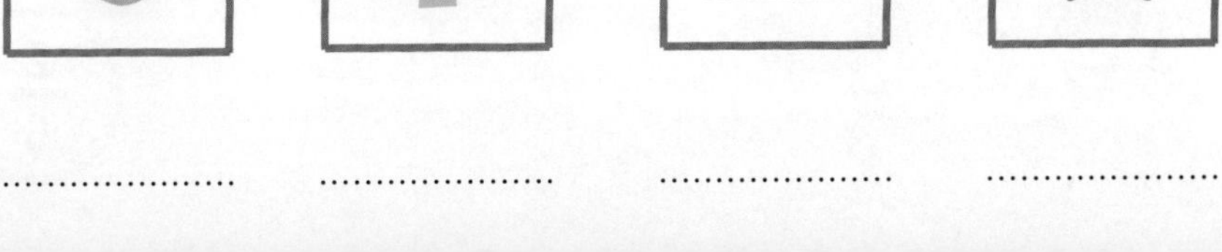

....

Picture parts

The dark area of each of these pictures represents a fraction of the whole picture. Draw a line to connect each picture to the fraction its shaded area represents.

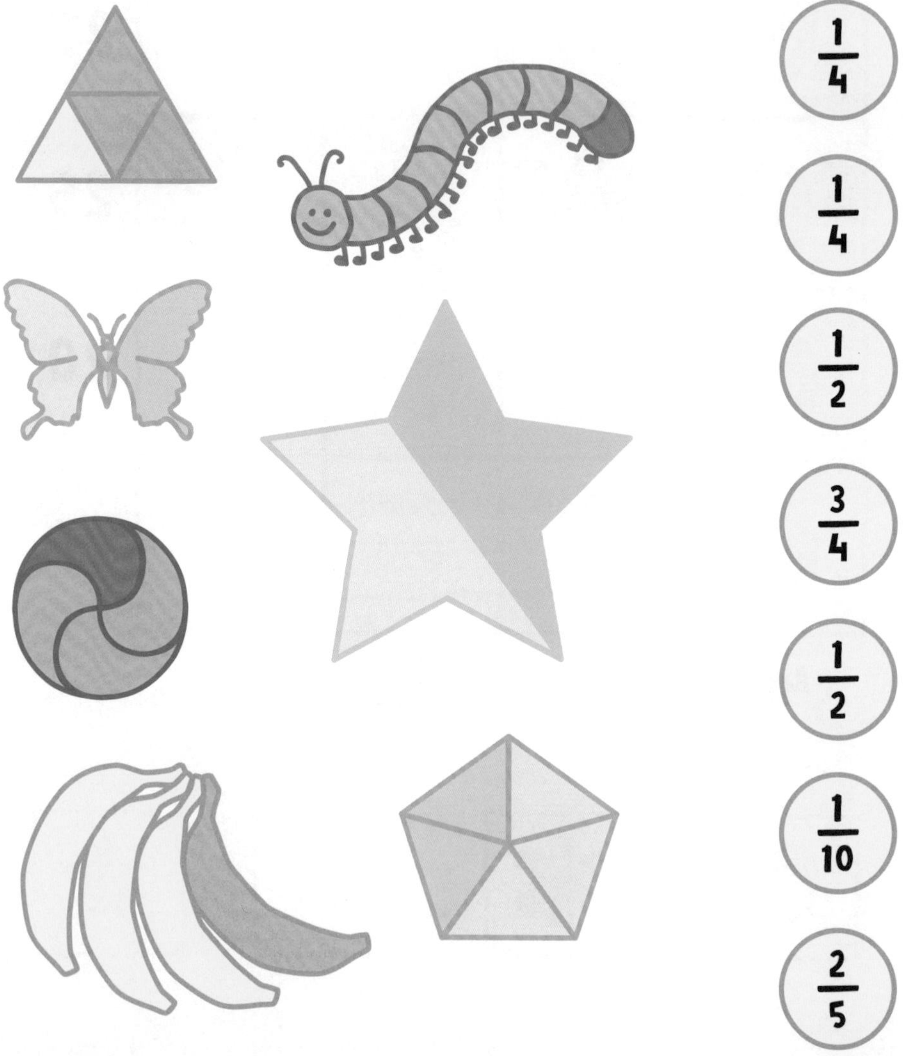

Microphone mix-up

Draw a circle around the microphone that is connected to the karaoke machine.

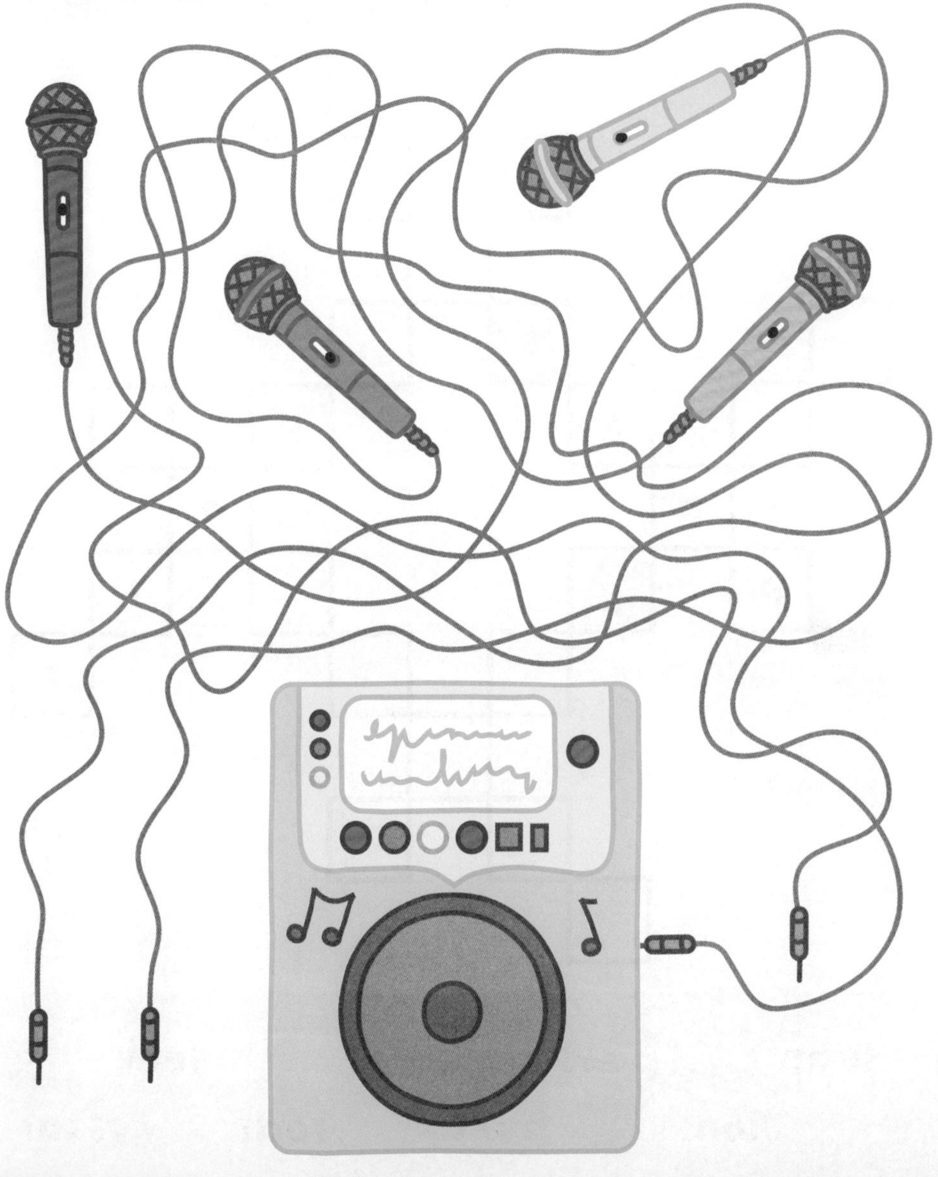

X-words

Fit the words below into the diagonal grid so that the last letter of one word is the first letter of another.

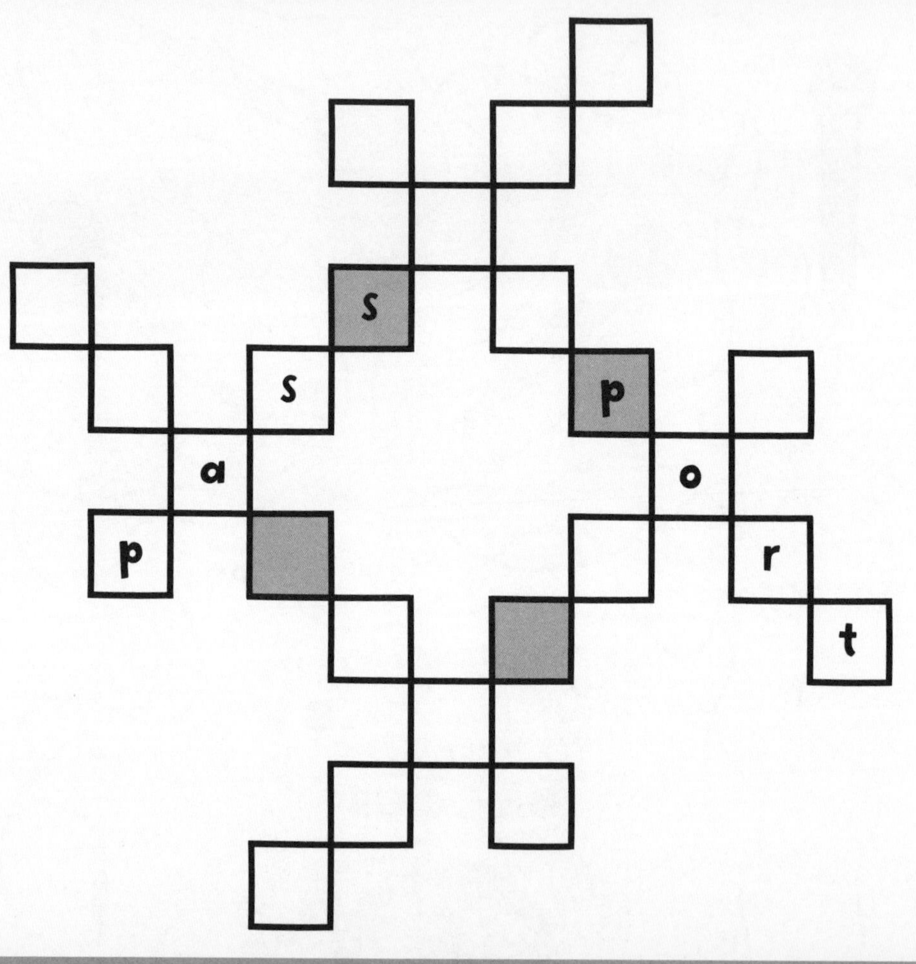

leap ~~pass~~ real seek

lion ~~port~~ roar star

Advanced archery

Who scored 25 points in the advanced archery contest?

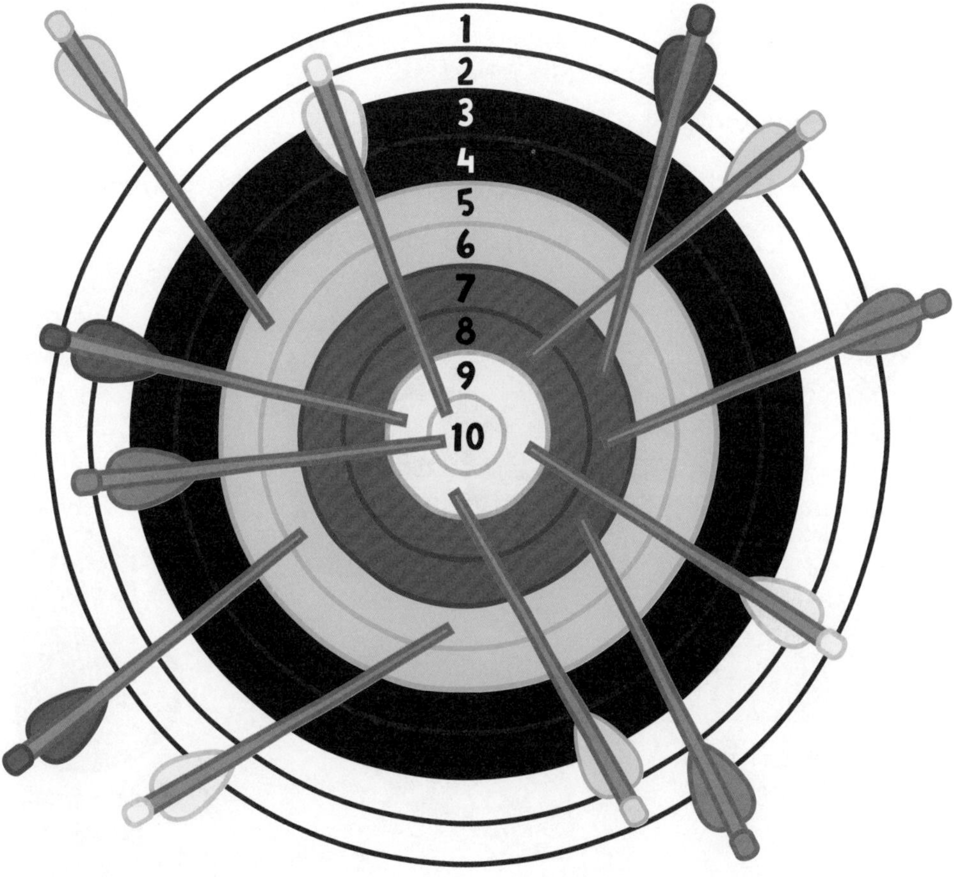

1
2
3
4
5
6
7
8
9
10

Scores:

William: ....

Robin: ....

Howard: ....

Artemis: ....

Souvenir shuffle

Use the clues below to work out who came home with which souvenir from abroad, then join them with lines.

- Amber's souvenir isn't red.
- Jake can't play his souvenir.
- The child with the shortest name has the souvenir from the country with the longest name.

Amber **Jake** **Louis** **Mei**

148

Alphablocks

Number the blocks at the bottom in alphabetical order, then copy their shapes into the grid to make a picture.

1.	2.	3.	4.	5.
6.	7.	8.	9.	10.
11.	12.	13.	14.	15.

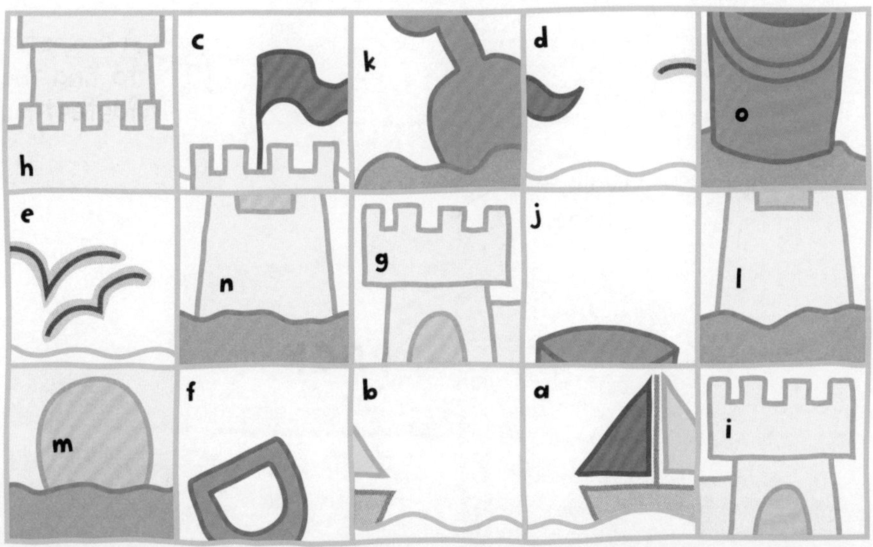

149 Word ladder

A word ladder is a puzzle that turns one word into another in several steps by changing one letter at a time. Use the clues around this word ladder to help you fill it in.

For example:

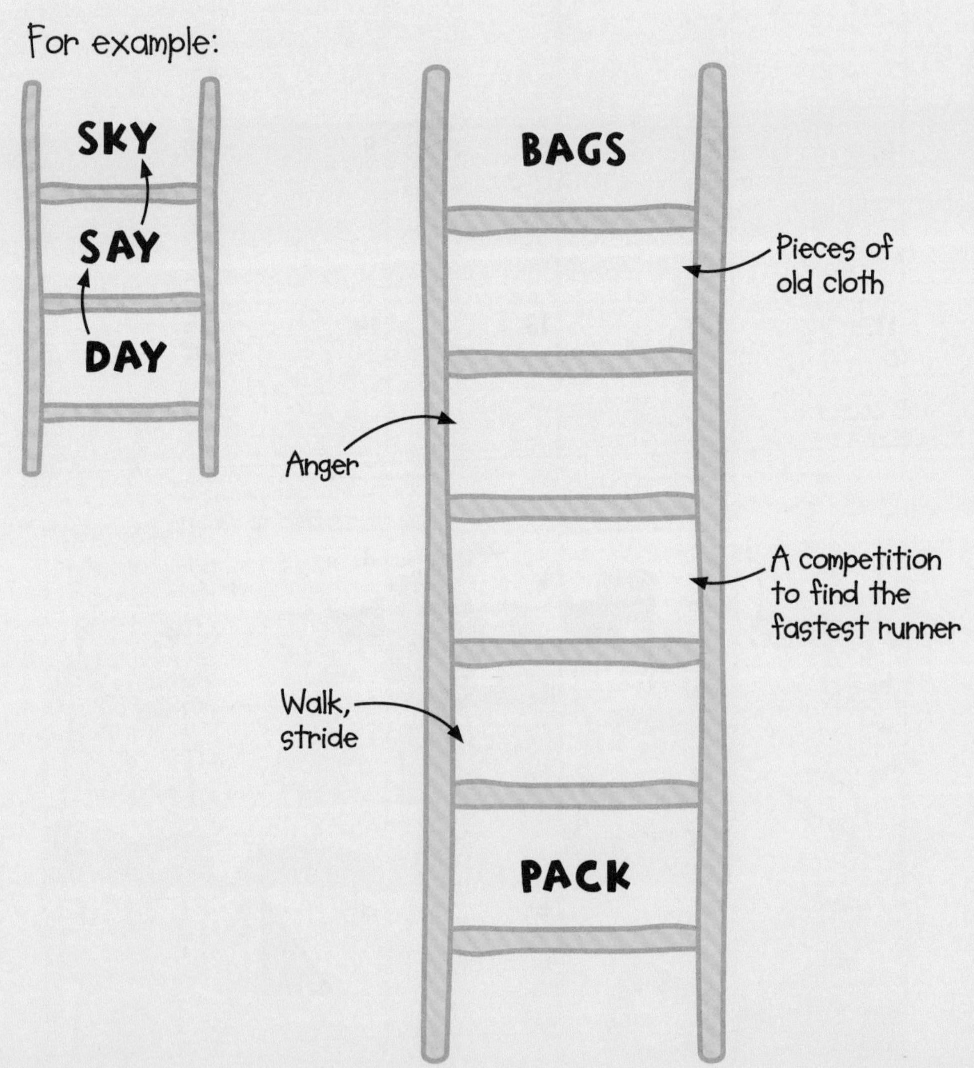

What goes where?

Try to fill the grid below so that each of the four pictures appears in every line, column, and block of four squares. Here is an example.

Crossnumber

	1			2	3	
4		5			6	
				7		
	8			9		10
11				12	13	
	14					

ACROSS CLUES

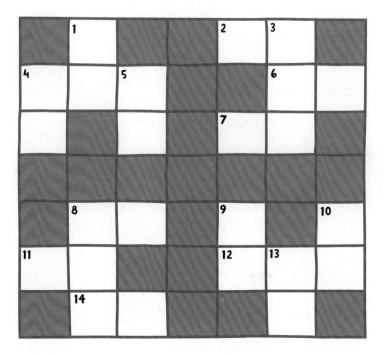

2. Unlucky number?
4. ___ Dalmatians
6. 11 × 6
7. Five times nine
8. Number of days in two weeks
11. A dozen
12. 6 across plus 7 across
14. 6 × 6

DOWN CLUES

1. 12 × 5
3. Number of days in a year
4. Four times four
5. A quarter of forty
8. "As easy as counting ___"
9. 10 down minus 5 down
10. 3 × 7
13. 14 across minus 10 down

Whose fish?

Follow the tangled fishing lines below to match the fishermen to their fish, and fill in each name next to his catch.

Rocky Andy Jimbo Johnny

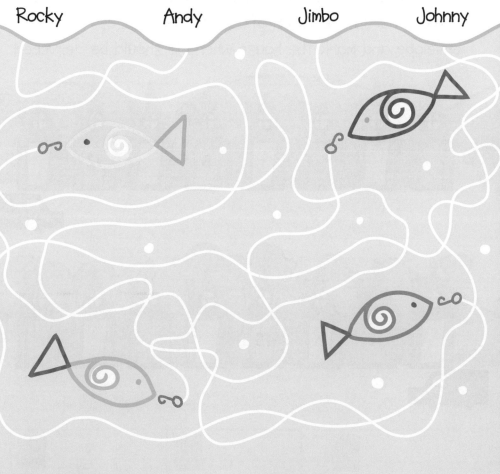

Yellow fish:.............................. Purple fish: ....

Green fish:.............................. Orange fish:..............................

153 House numbers

The house numbers on Even Street go up in even numbers. The house numbers on Odd Lane go up in odd numbers. Only two houses in each row have a number on the door – the others have fallen off. Read the address on each envelope and mark the house where it should be delivered.

Mr. Joe Smith
17, Odd Lane

A.

Miss. Amy Brown
4, Even Street

B.

Mrs. Pam Davies
23, Odd Lane

C.

X-words

Fit the words below into the diagonal grid so that the last letter of one word is the first letter of another.

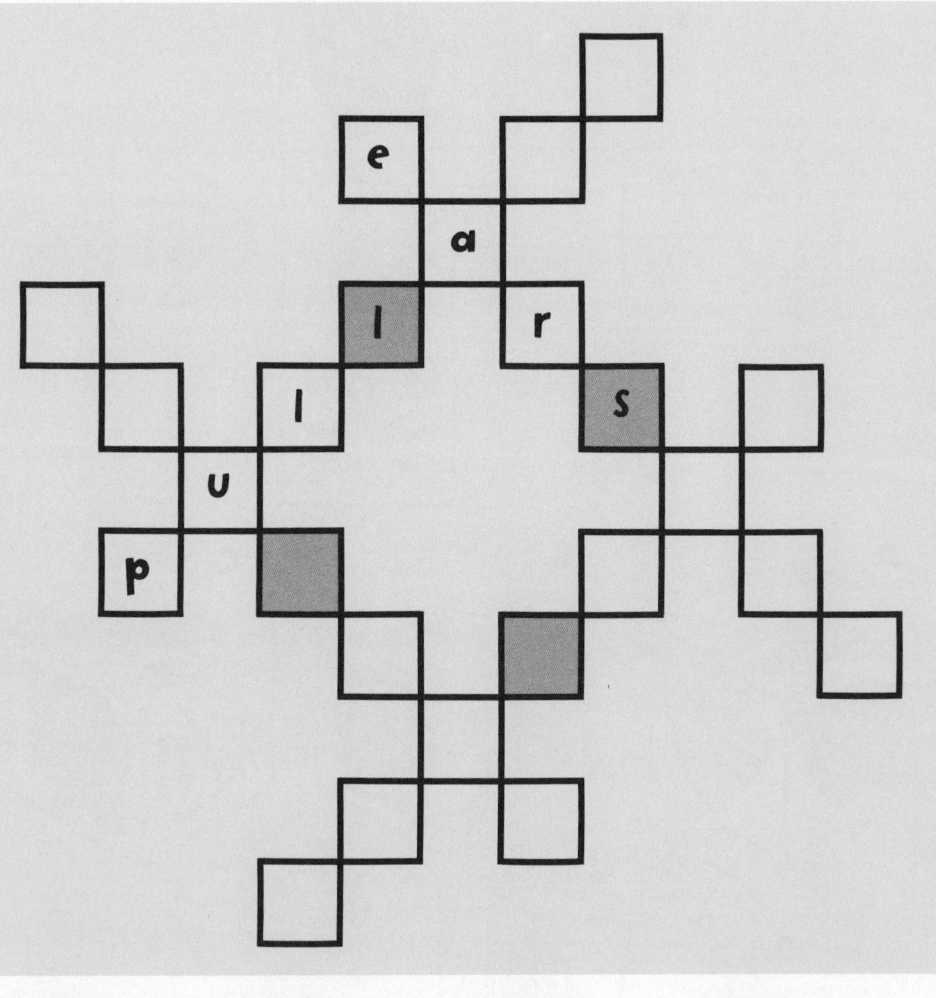

coin **hour** **nail** **rain**

~~ears~~ **lark** **~~pull~~** **sing**

155

Ocean cube

Which two picture cubes can be made from the unfolded net below?

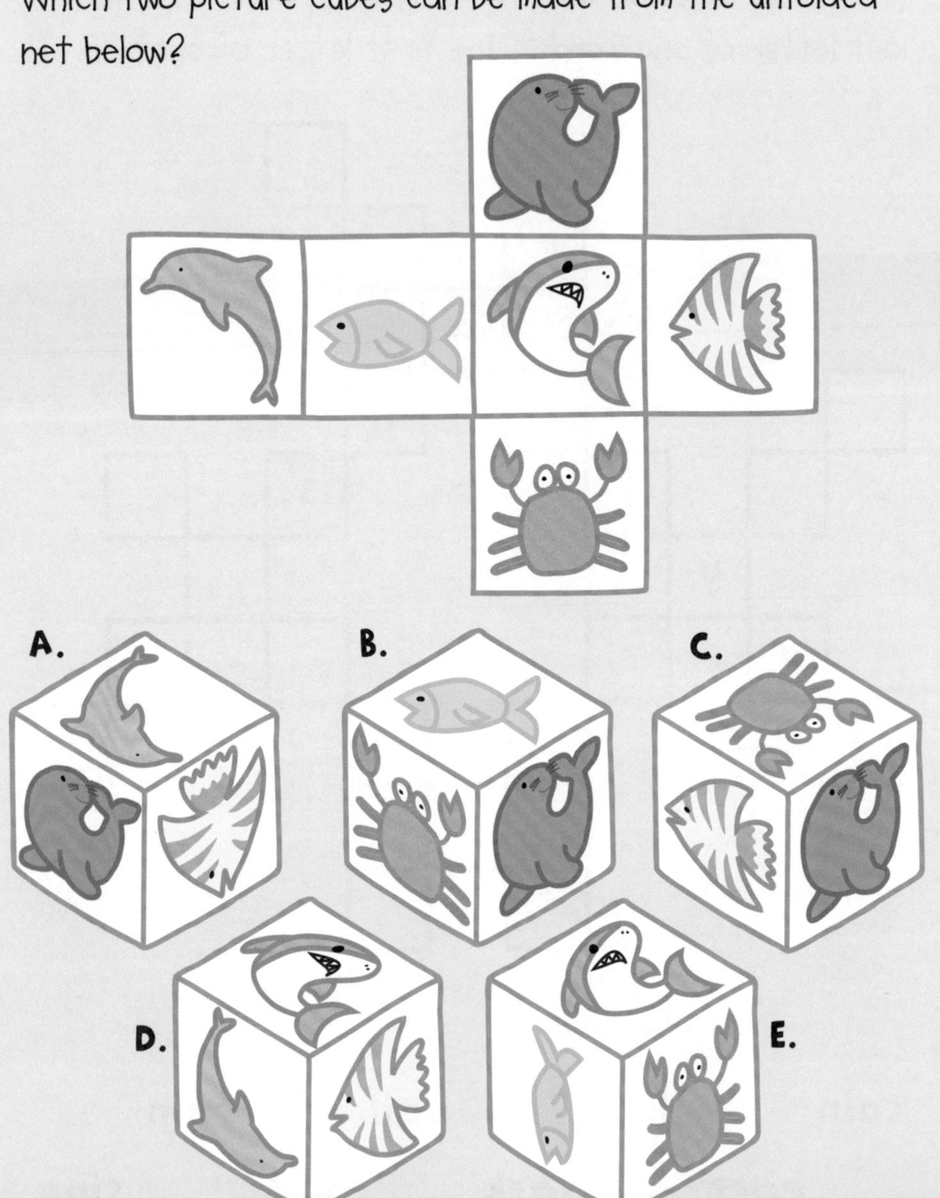

Double vision

Copy the drawings across into the blank spaces to see two complete pictures of flowers and buzzing bees.

Odd ones out

Draw a circle around the odd one out in each row.

1.    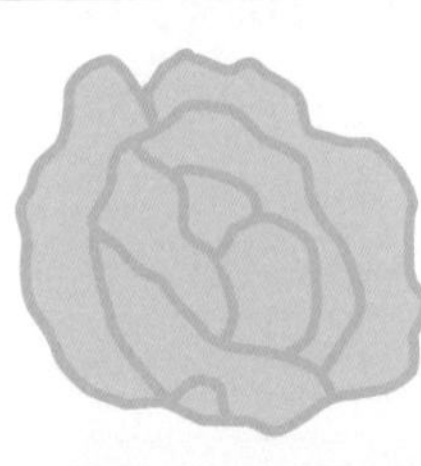 

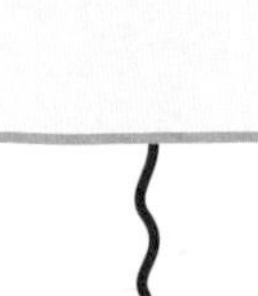 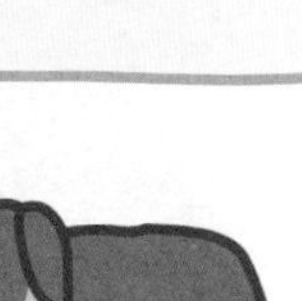

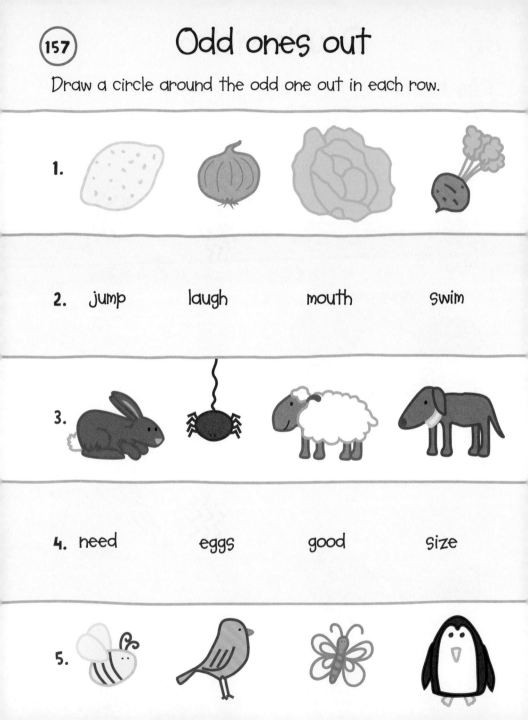

2. jump laugh mouth swim

3.    

4. need eggs good size

5.   

Toothpaste tangle

It's time for Ernie the alligator to brush his teeth. Which line will lead him to his tube of toothpaste?

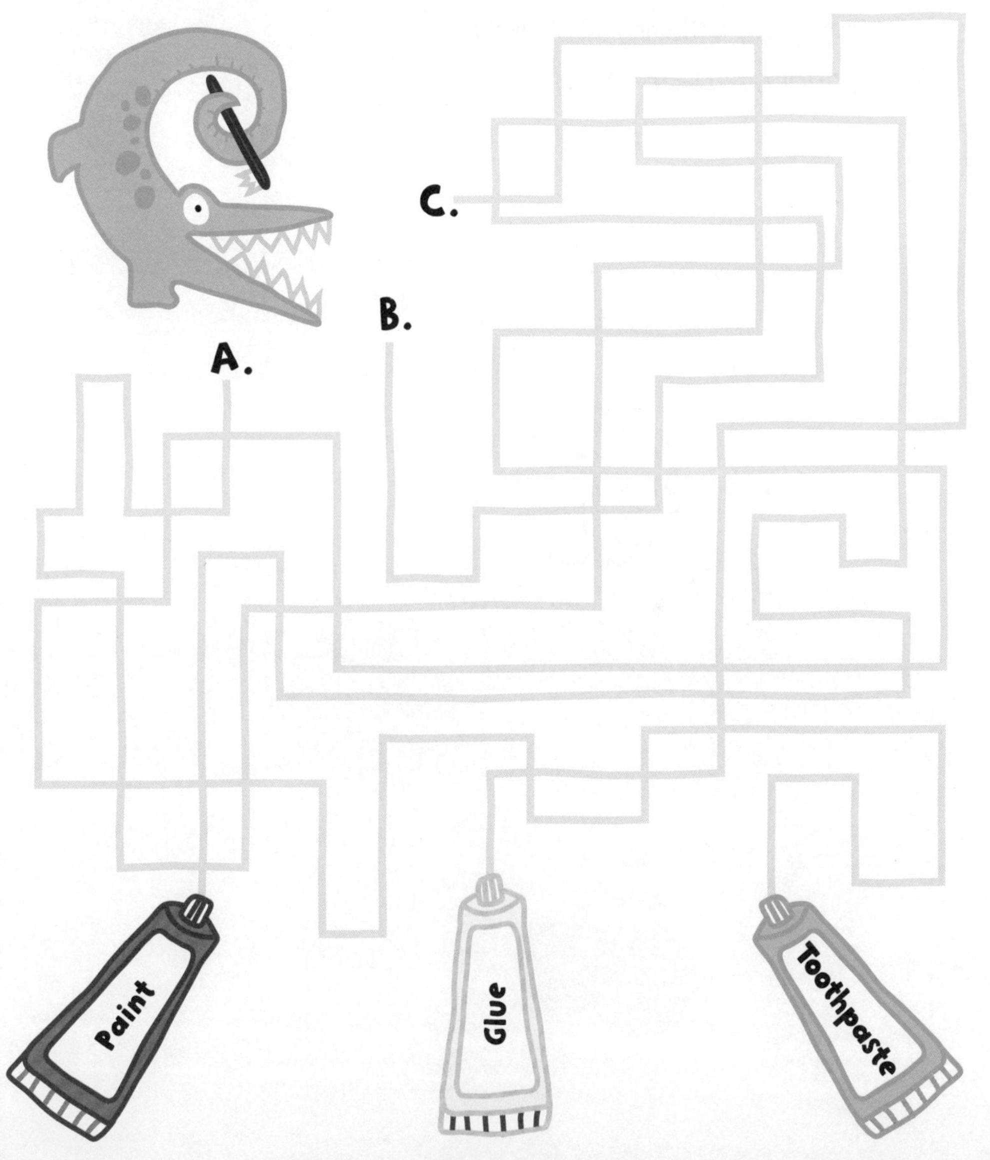

What goes where?

Try to fill the grid below so that each of the four pictures appears in every line, column, and block of four squares. Here is an example.

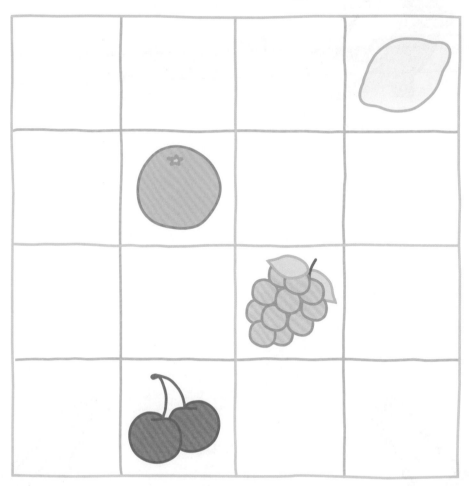

Beach picture

Follow these instructions to complete the beach picture below:

- Draw a sun **above** the seagull.
- Draw a beach ball **under** the palm tree.
- Draw a bucket **next** to the sandcastle.
- Draw a straw **inside** the glass.

161 Where am I going?

Follow the trails to find out where each person is going on a trip:

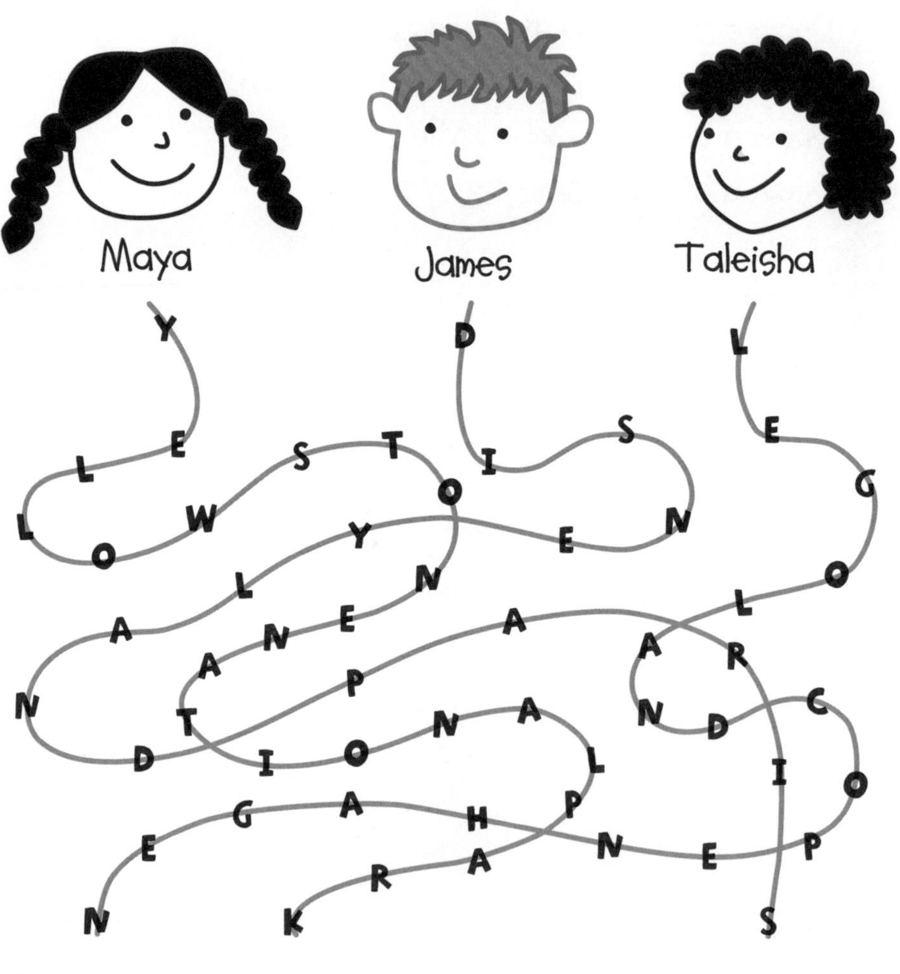

James: ....

Maya: ....

Taleisha: ....

Where do they eat...?

Beneath each food, write the name of the country where it is famously eaten.

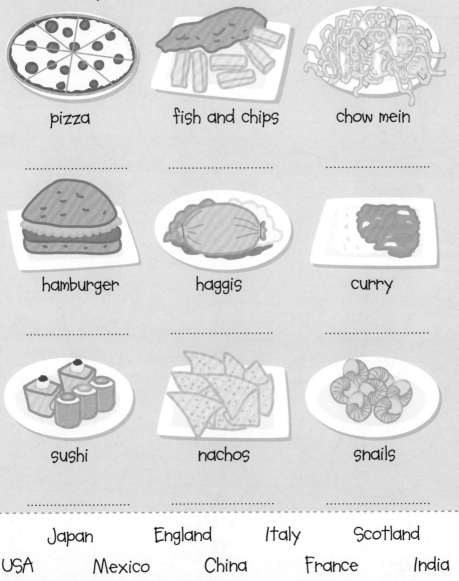

Japan England Italy Scotland

USA Mexico China France India

163

How many dinosaurs?

How many prehistoric creatures can you count here?

Answer: ....

Polar alphabet

An explorer is trying to translate a mysterious message carved on an igloo near the North Pole. Use the guide to the Polar alphabet to help him translate it into English.

Nᐁᒥᔪᐱᒪᐁ ᑕᐱ ᑕHᐁ ᓇᐱᕋᑕH ᐸᐱᒥᐁ

ᐃ ᐊᒪ ᐊNᐊᐯ ᕗᐃᓴHᐃᓇᒐ ᕕᐅᑕ ᕗᐁᐁᒥ

ᕗᕋᐁᐁ ᑕᐱ ᓴHᐁᒥᑕᐁᕋ ᐃᓇ ᒪᐯ ᐃᒐᒥᐱᐱ

ᕕᐁᓴᑕ NᐃᓴHᐁᓴ

ᕗᕋᐱᒪ ᑲᐱᐱᒥᐃᑲ

ᐊ	ᕕ	ᔪ	ᑎ	ᐁ	ᕗ	ᒐ	H	ᐃ	ᑲ	ᒥ
a	b	c	d	e	f	g	h	i	k	l

ᒪ	ᓇ	ᐱ	ᐸ	ᕋ	ᓴ	ᑕ	ᐅ	N	ᐯ
m	n	o	p	r	s	t	u	w	y

165 It's all Greek to me

Can you read what the writing says on this Ancient Greek vase? (Clue: think of a snake)

Calculate this!

See if you can find the solution to this giant calculation.

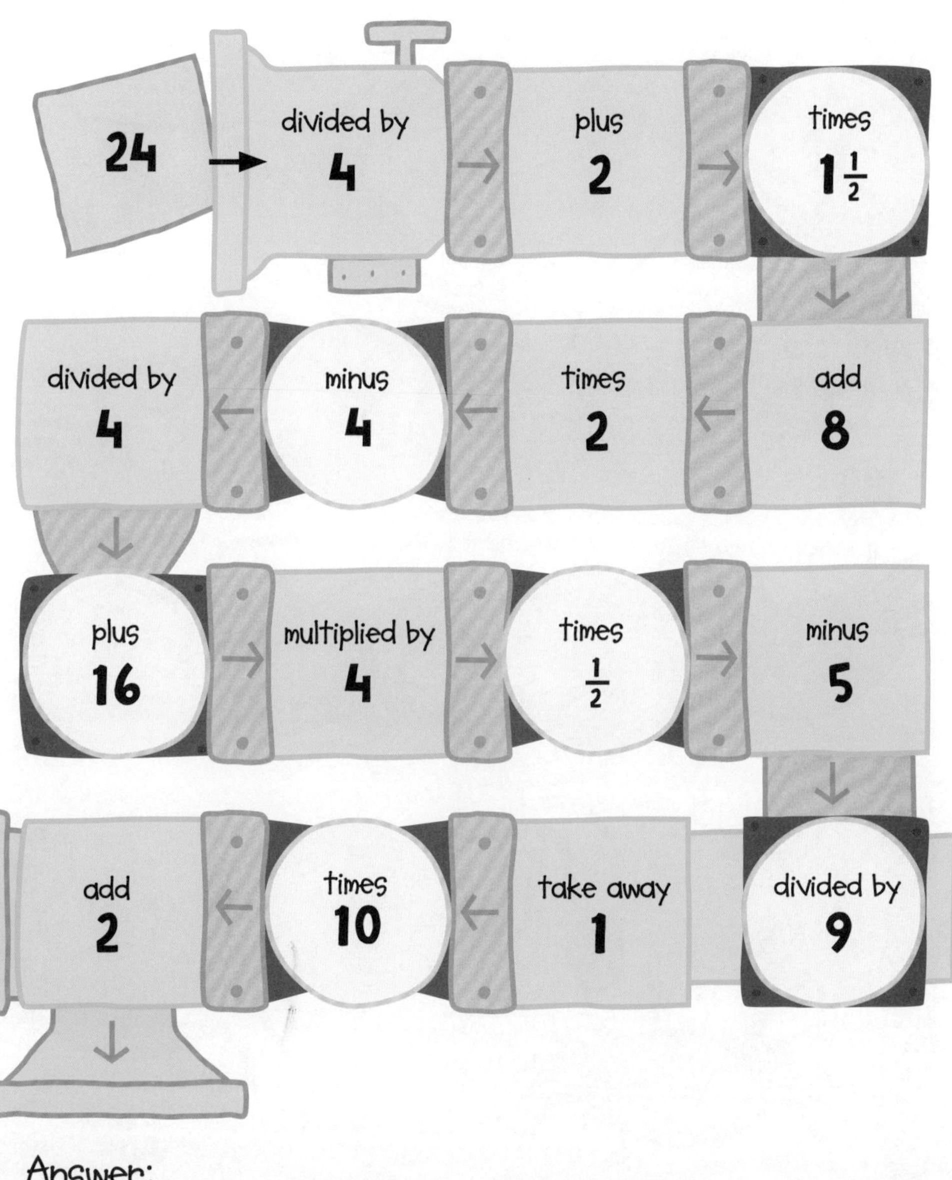

Answer: ....

Odd crab out

Draw a circle around the crab that is the odd one out.

Starting grid

Copy the racing car below into the larger grid, so that it is drawn at double the size.

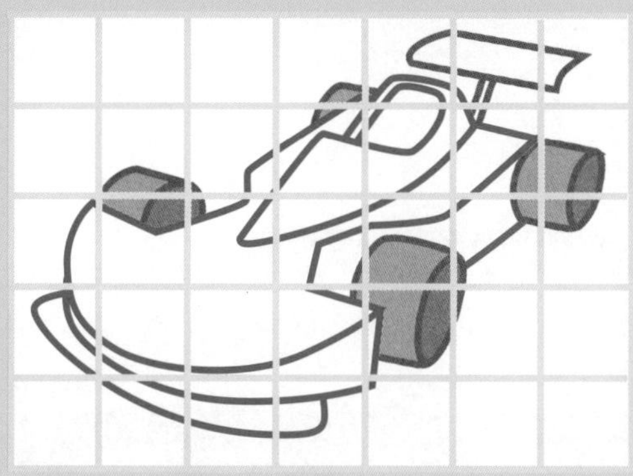

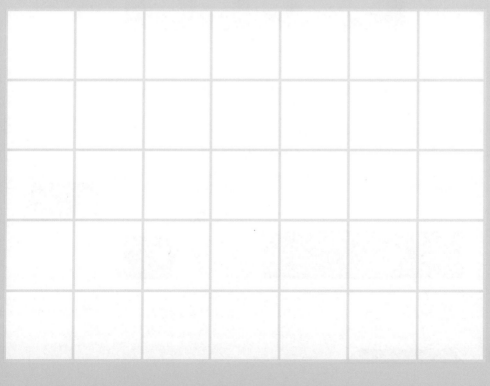

Ship shapes

Draw a circle around each shape at the bottom of the page that has not been used to make this picture.

Animal cube

Which one of the picture cubes can be made from the unfolded net below?

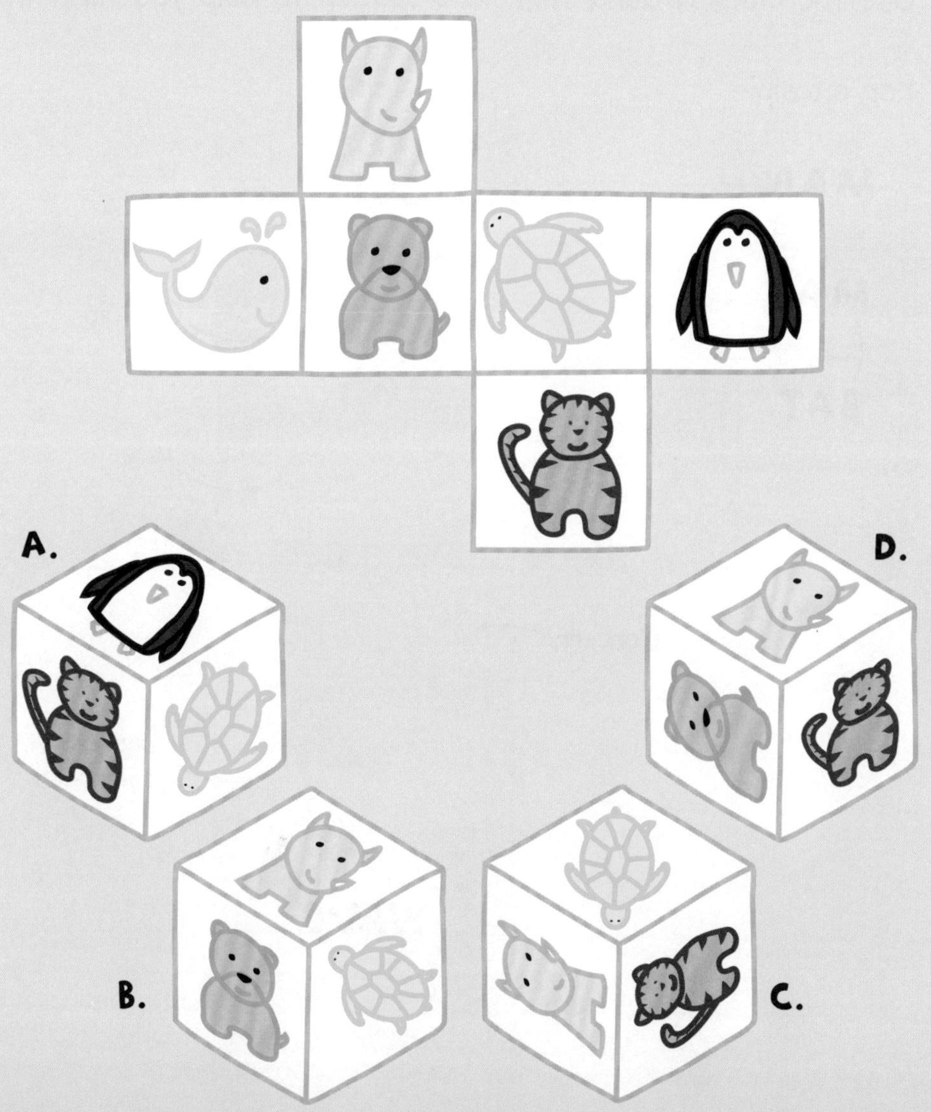

171 Word ladder

A word ladder is a puzzle that turns one word into another in several steps by changing one letter at a time. Use the clues around this word ladder to help you fill it in.

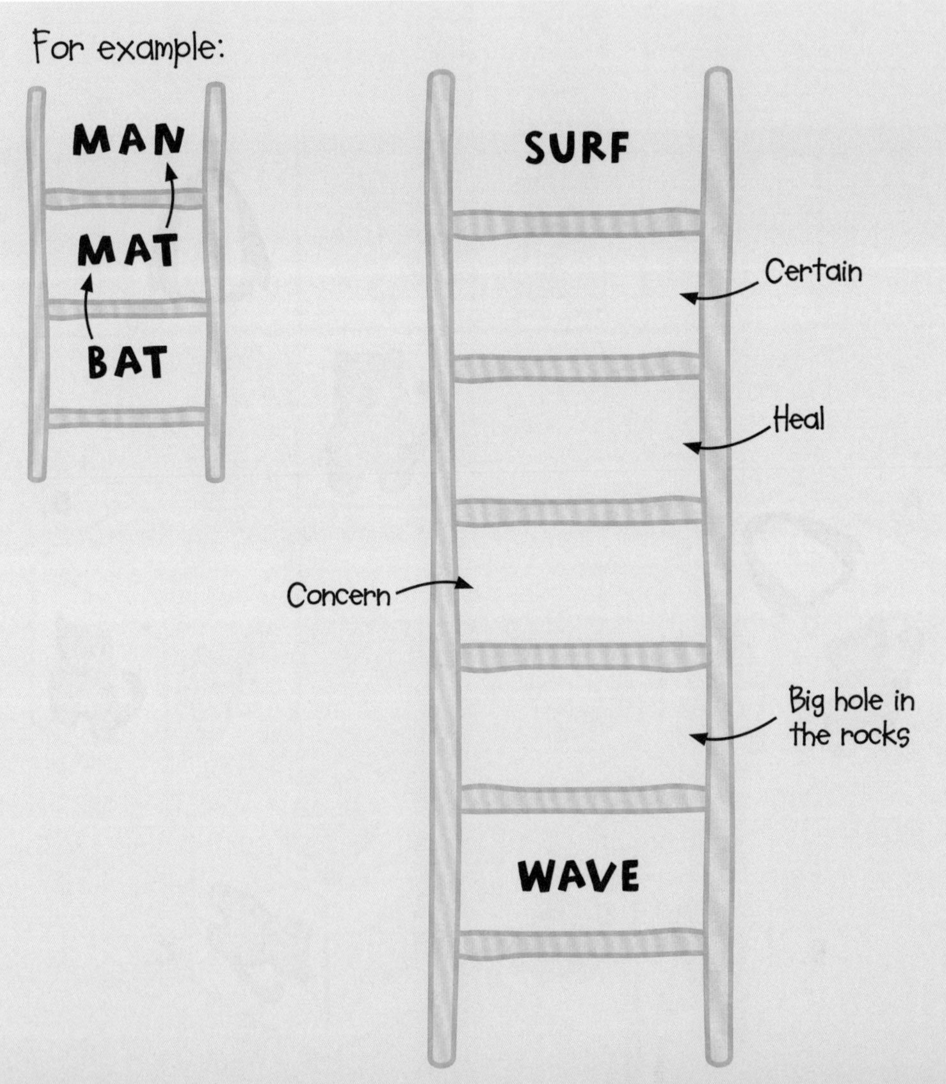

Planet puzzle

Put the planets in order of size from smallest to largest, not including rings. Which planet's name is hidden in the first letters of your answer?

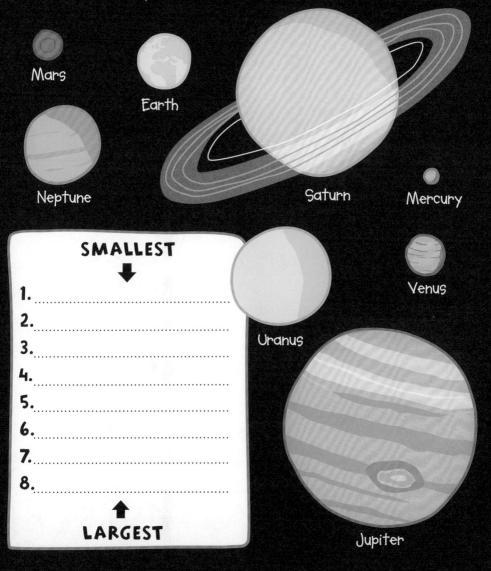

Mars

Earth

Neptune

Saturn

Mercury

Uranus

Venus

SMALLEST

1. ....
2. ....
3. ....
4. ....
5. ....
6. ....
7. ....
8. ....

LARGEST

Jupiter

173

Busy bees

Find the pattern in the path each bee is taking as it moves from flower to flower. Draw a 'P' over the flower each bee will visit next.

Counting squares

How many squares can you find in this pattern?

Answer: ....

Bus trip

175

Three buses are carrying a total of one hundred tourists. The blue bus is carrying ten more tourists than the red bus. The red bus is carrying thirty fewer tourists than the green bus. How many tourists is each bus carrying? Write the correct number next to each one.

Magical creatures

Try to find all the magical creatures below hidden in the grid. They may be written in any direction.

u	n	h	a	h	d	x	u	o	y	p
g	r	i	f	f	i	n	g	i	d	b
f	r	p	i	n	r	g	r	s	r	d
n	a	p	e	g	a	s	u	s	a	s
n	r	o	c	i	n	u	p	h	g	o
v	h	g	n	e	r	p	n	f	o	n
p	i	r	f	n	s	r	n	h	n	n
d	r	i	b	r	e	d	n	u	h	t
g	v	f	y	v	o	v	b	n	p	p
f	p	f	y	h	p	c	t	f	n	r
o	i	w	b	e	w	r	o	c	p	w

dragon	griffin	phoenix	hippogriff
wyvern	unicorn	pegasus	thunderbird

Daisy Rabbit

Help Daisy Rabbit find her sisters in their warren.

Greater, less or equal?

Fill in the missing symbols to make each line true. Use < for "less than", > for "more than" or = for "is equal to".

1. the number of days in a month  the number of months in a year

2. the number of toes on a foot  the number of legs on a spider

3. the number of wheels on a car  the number of sides on a square

4. the number of thirds in a whole  the number of singers in a duet

5. the number of letters in the alphabet  the number of minutes in half an hour

Back words

Find nine words that you can write backward to match the meanings below. For example, 'pots' is 'stop' backward.

hay **warts** **loots** **straw** **swap** **mined** **strap** **guns** **stench** **moor** **stun** **drawer** **gulp** **spool** **knits** **brag** **wolf**

1. Chair without a back or arms ....
2. Sections ....
3. Cloth used in jeans ....
4. Dried wheat stalks ....
5. Stopper for sink or bathtub ....
6. Prize ....
7. Bad smell ....
8. A dog's feet ....
9. Comfortable ....

Robot symmetry

Three of these robots are symmetrical – if you draw a line down the middle of their bodies, the sides will match each other like a reflection in a mirror. Draw circles around the three symmetrical robots.

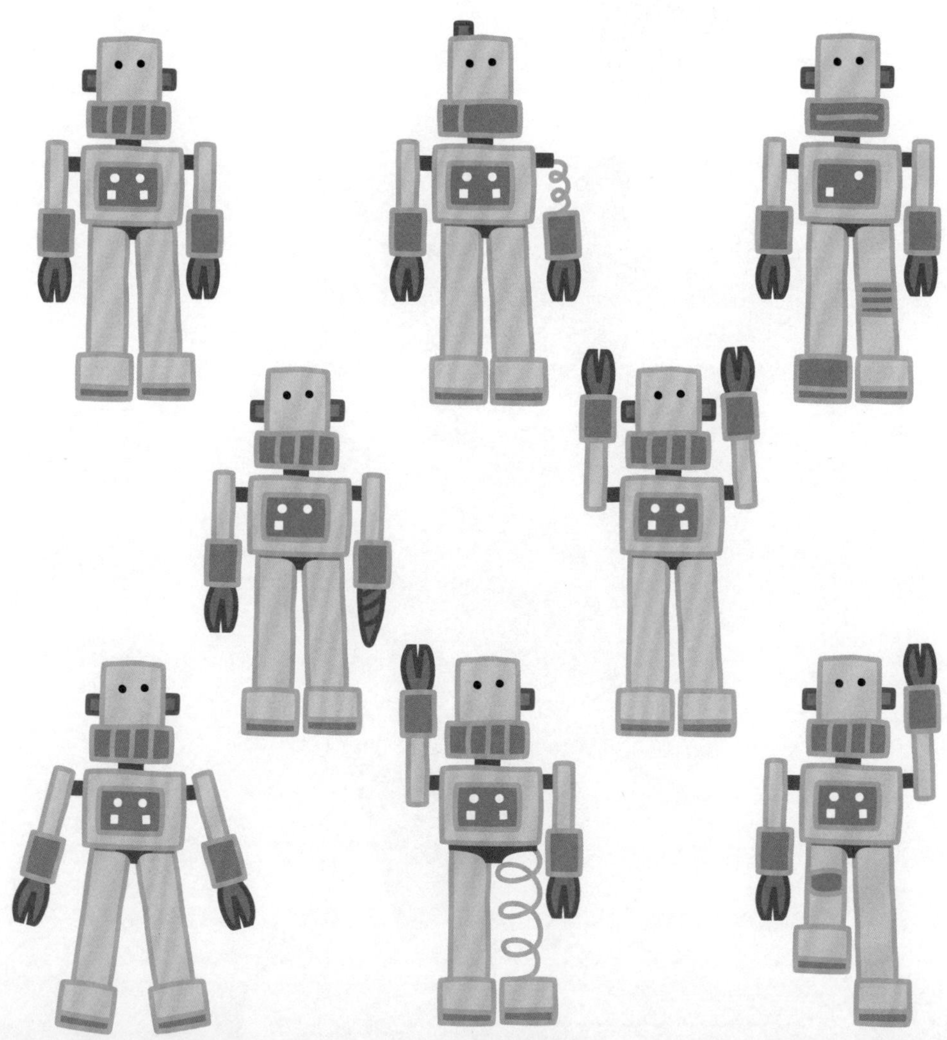

181

Counting diamonds

How many diamond shapes can you see in this kite?

Answer: ....

Back to front

Find out the time on each clock by looking at these reflections. Write the correct answer under each clock.

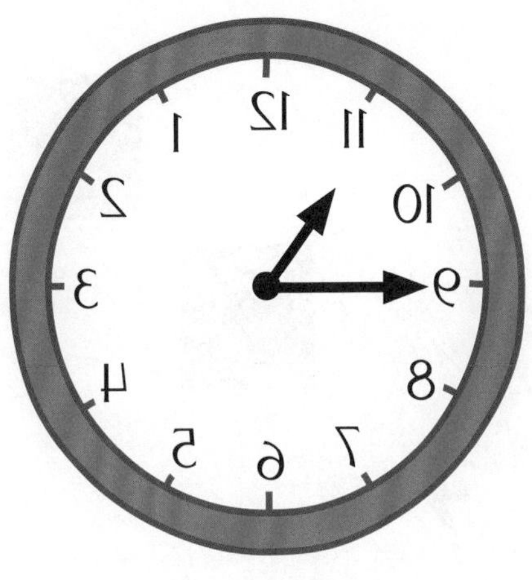

10:45

A.

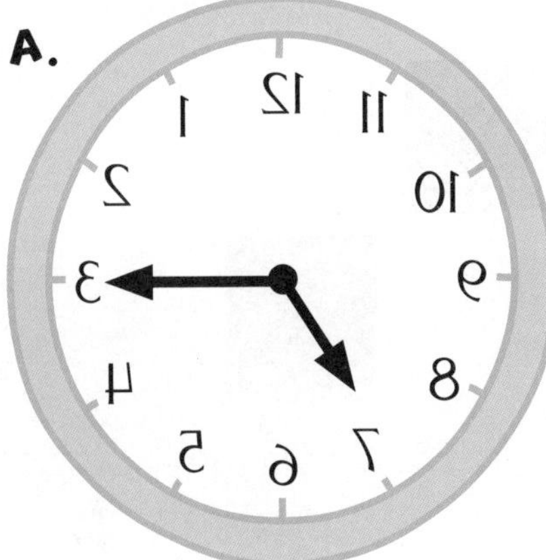

....

B.

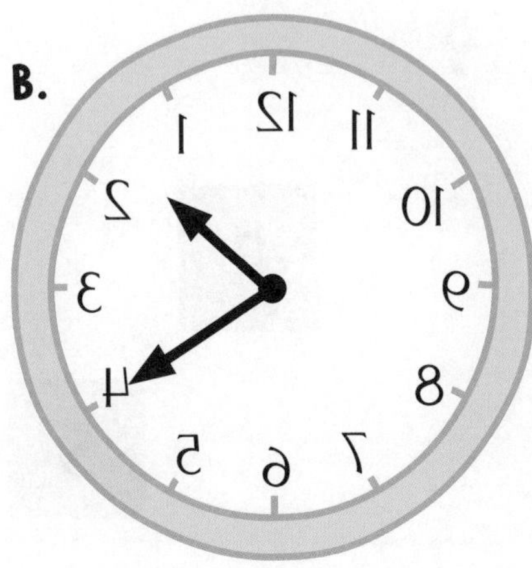

....

C.

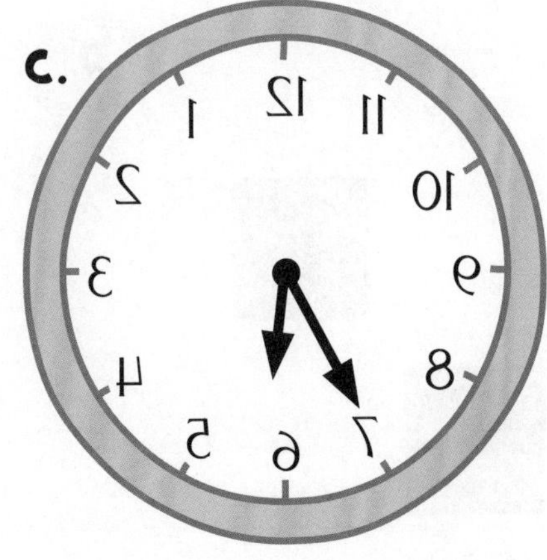

....

183

Highest total

What is the highest total you can make by adding only five numbers that are joined by blue lines? You can start at any number, but you can't skip one, or use one twice.

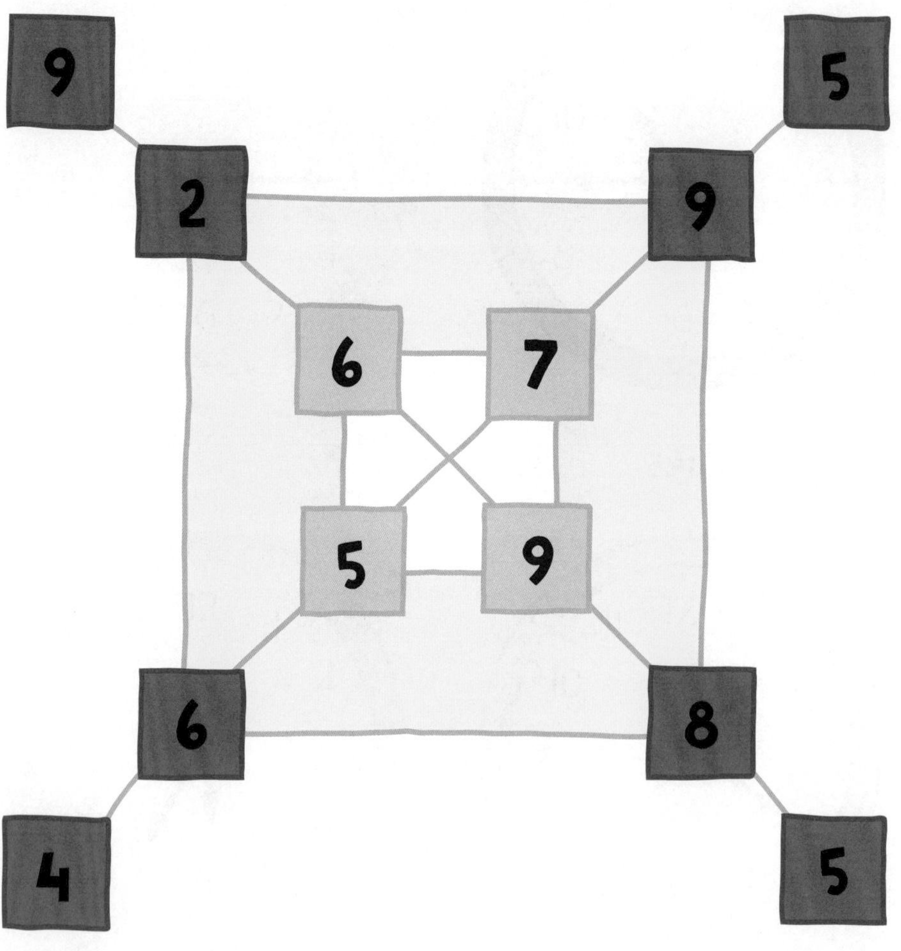

Answer: ....

Bake the cake

Number the circles to put this sequence in the right order to make and bake the cake.

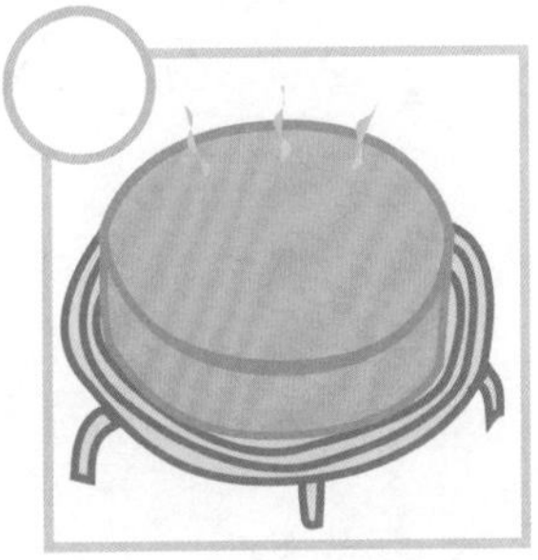

Moon flight

Join up the dots to see what's whizzing past the Moon.

Missing letters

Some letters in the message below have been replaced by seaside pictures. Try to find out which letter each picture stands for, and read the message.

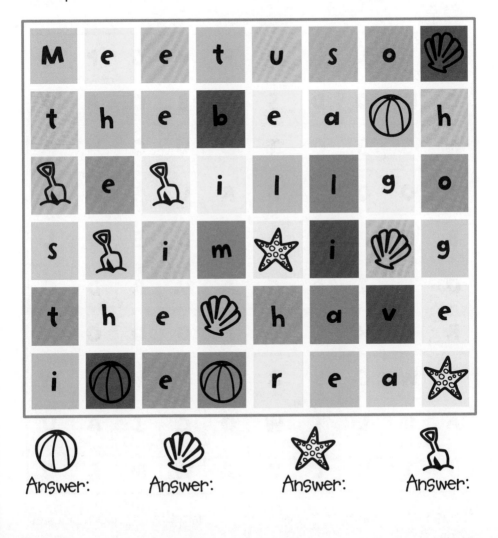

M	e	e	t	u	s	o	
t	h	e	b	e	a		h
	e		i	l	l	g	o
s		i	m		i		g
t	h	e		h	a	v	e
i		e		r	e	a	

Answer: ....

Answer: ....

Answer: ....

Answer: ....

Birdsearch

Find the names of the birds below hidden in the grid. They may be written in any direction.

A	U	L	L	P	P	R	G	P	S
C	W	O	D	S	W	B	O	A	W
N	S	S	O	T	O	U	O	W	A
I	O	O	T	H	R	U	S	H	L
B	U	Z	Z	A	R	D	E	O	L
O	E	I	P	G	A	M	R	D	O
R	E	K	C	E	P	D	O	O	W
I	W	G	S	R	S	P	B	W	W
A	O	L	T	W	O	C	I	A	U
J	I	R	L	H	Z	W	N	R	O

thrush robin owl magpie woodpecker
swallow crow sparrow goose buzzard

Coconut shy

The number under each coconut shows how many points you score for knocking it down. You may knock down each coconut only once.

1. What's the lowest score you can make by knocking down three coconuts?

Answer:..

2. What's the highest score you can make by knocking down three coconuts?

Answer:..

3. What's the smallest number of coconuts you need to knock down to score 25 points?

Answer:..

See-saws

A doll weighs twice as much as a teddy bear, and a toy dinosaur weighs twice as much as a doll.

1. How many teddy bears would you need to put on the empty end of this see-saw to make it balanced?

Answer:...

2. How many dolls would you need to put on the empty end of this see-saw to make it balanced?

Answer:...

Secret code

This secret spy message has been written in code.
Use the key below to decode the message.

Vmvnb hkrvh szev hvvm gsilfts blfi wrhtfrhv. Ivgfim gl gsv hvxivg yzhv zh hllm zh blf xzm.

a	b	c	d	e	f	g	h	i	j	k	l	m
n	o	p	q	r	s	t	u	v	w	x	y	z

Key: ZYX Code a=z, b=y, c=x, and so on

Whose baby?

Draw lines to match the adult animals with their young.

Horse	Puppy
Goat	Duckling
Dog	Piglet
Duck	Calf
Pig	Fawn
Bear	Cub
Butterfly	Kid
Cow	Foal
Deer	Caterpillar

Butterfly maze

Help the butterfly through the maze to reach the flower.

193

Puzzle search

Which is the missing piece of the jigsaw puzzle?

A.

B.

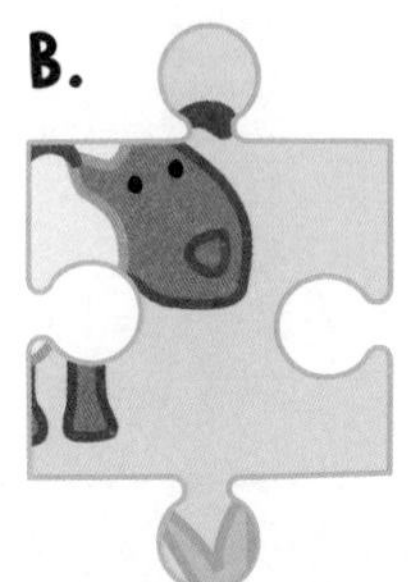

C.

D.

Hickory Dickory

Draw the hands on the clocks in the right positions, then draw lines between hands that point toward each other to make a route for the mouse to get to the cheese.

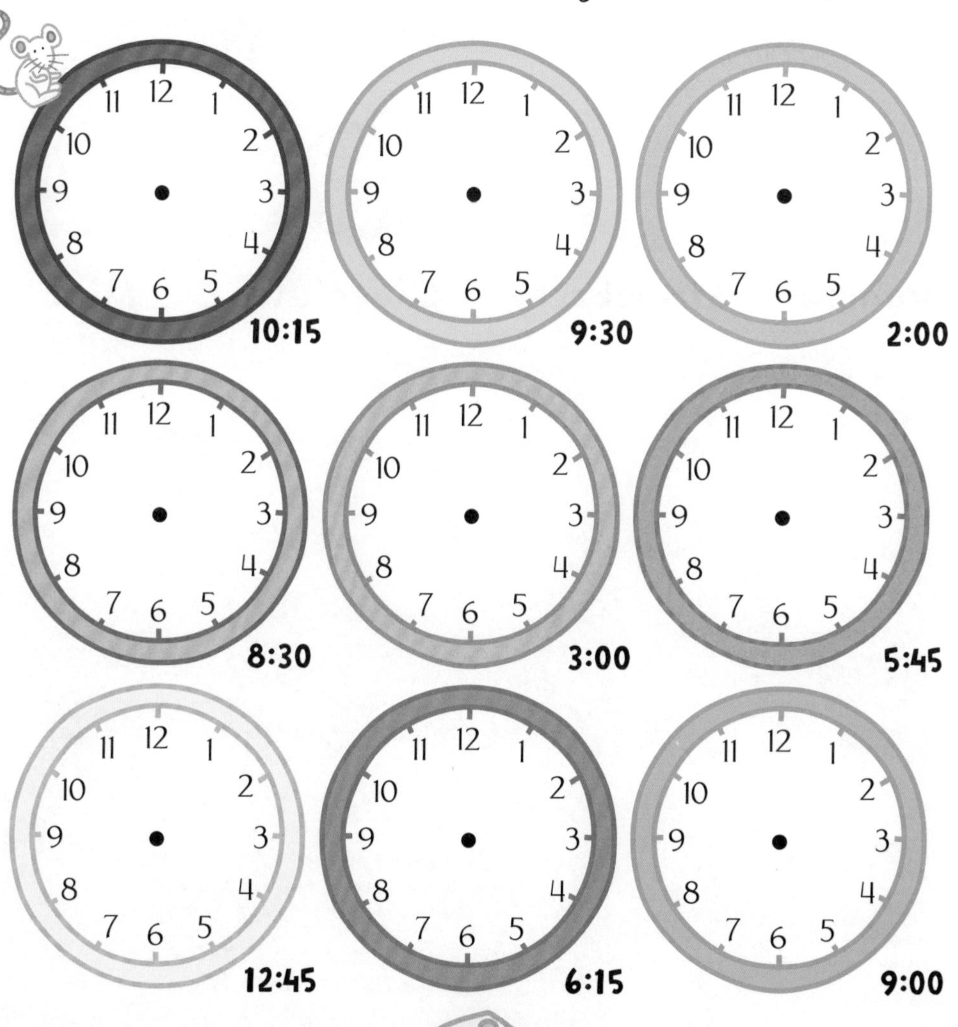

195

Gino's Ice Creams

Gino sells four types of ice cream. If there are two scoops in each cone, how many combinations can he make that contain two different types? You can use the empty cones to try your combinations.

Answer: ....

Back to the start

Find out which set of instructions was used to draw the shape, then circle the dot where the drawing began.

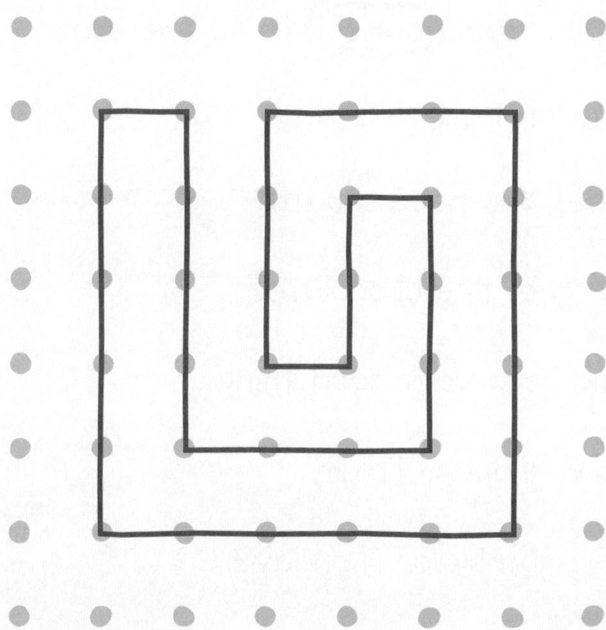

1. right 3, down 5, left 5, up 4, right 1, down 4, right 3, up 3, left 1, down 2, left 1, up 3.

2. right 1, up 2, right 1, down 3, left 3, up 4, left 1, down 5, right 5, up 5, left 3, down 3.

3. right 1, down 4, right 3, up 3, left 1, down 3, left 1, up 3, right 3, down 5, left 5, up 5.

197 Hidden animals

See if you can find the names of the animals pictured below. One is hidden in each sentence.

For example: Anna **came l**ate to the show.

1. I hope I don't catch a cold.

2. Phoo-ee! You need a bath.

3. Why do girls like chocolate?

4. It would be a very good thing.

5. Eat your grapes, Tommy.

6. Shall we go now or Monday?

198

Ski slope

Draw the path the skier should follow down the slope so that he only passes between flags with odd numbers.

Answers

1. Pencil pick-up:
B, C, A, G, F, E, D

2. Honeycomb hexagons:

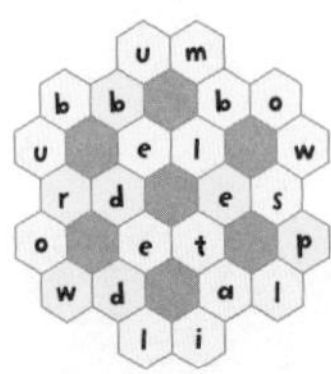

3. Number monster:
1. 4x7=28 2. 5x4=20
3. 8x3=24

4. Patchwork puzzle:

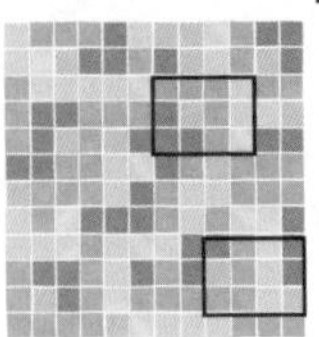

5. Hiss!: python

6. Baggage tags:

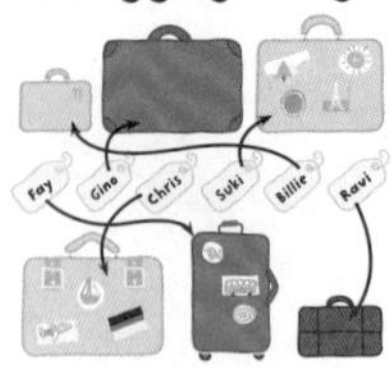

7. Who?:

9. Word cross:
1. P 2. A 3. L 4. R

10. Odd one out: C

11. Apple maze:

12. Spot the spots: 24

13. Celebration: birthday

14. Square numbers:

2	6	12
4	8	16
6	10	20

15. Dinosaur digits:
Blue (+5): 5..15...35.45..
Orange (+4): 4...20,24.32,36..

16. Spot the difference:

17. Word count: dragon

18. Missing cookies:
1. 4 2. 2 3. 1

19. Necks letter:
1. C,F,H 2. P,V,X 3. Y,V,T

20. Mini-sudoku:

3	4	2	1
2	1	3	4
1	2	4	3
4	3	1	2

21. Crossword:

22. Strawberry sundaes:
1. 2 2. 4 3. 4

23. Confused words:
1. ✓ 2. ✓ 3. ✗ 4. ✓ 5. ✓ 6. ✗ 7. ✗

24. Number trains:
1. 5+7=12 2. 8−5=3
3. 3x4=12 4. 27÷3=9
5. 4x5=20

25. Magic square:

8	1	6
3	5	7
4	9	2

26. Avoid the asteroids:

27. Mini-sudoku:

1	3	2	4
4	2	3	1
2	1	4	3
3	4	1	2

28. How many birds: 17

29. What goes where?:

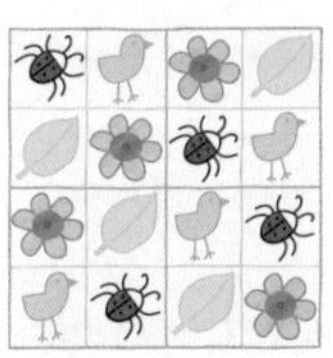

30. Picture letter:
Dear Henry, I was very happy to hear from you on my birthday. Thank you for my slippers. Lots of love from Grandpa XXX

31. Counting triangles: 23

32. Toy box: 1. red 2. 3 3. no 4. the robot 5. ABCDE 6. right

33. Honeycomb hexagons:

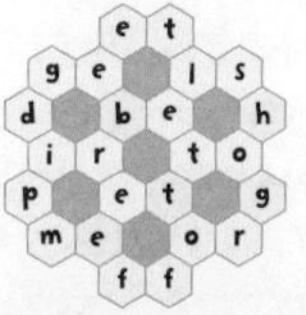

34. Rupanapi Island:

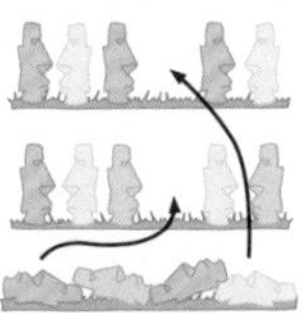

35. Under the sea:

36. Find the dogs:

R	E	L	D	O	O	P	N	L	L	H	C	W
O	I	L	A	B	B	R	C	H	R	W	K	C
U	E	E	L	B	T	U	N	G	H	O	C	A
G	N	I	M	B	R	L	L	Y	C	H	S	O
H	A	E	A	O	D	A	B	L	A	C	Y	O
C	D	N	T	I	B	S	D	L	D	W	D	U
O	T	H	I	K	I	E	S	O	W	O	B	D
L	A	O	A	S	O	R	A	S	R	H	G	O
L	E	I	N	A	P	S	R	E	K	C	O	C
I	R	B	E	A	G	L	E	B	N	S	O	A
E	G	R	E	Y	H	O	U	N	D	W	D	R
P	A	A	D	O	C	B	W	S	I	R	P	I
L	C	G	E	N	T	H	D	K	D	E	S	D

37. Confused countries:
1. Turkey 2. Germany 3. France 4. Portugal 5. China 6. Great Britain 7. Mexico 8. United States 9. Poland 10. South Africa

38. Hidden picture:

39. Directions: Red: Apple Rd Yellow: Ink St Green: Green St

41. Triangle art:

42. Birds on a wire:

43. Shredded words:

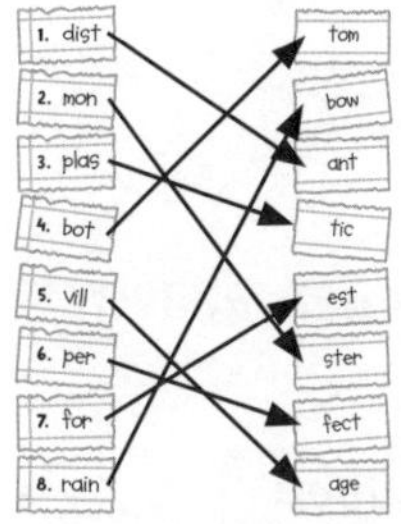

44. Apple picking:

45. Sticker selection:
1. 3 2. 4

46. Dog show:
A. Biggest: 3rd Longest hair: 3rd Most spots: 1st; B. Biggest: 1st Longest hair: 2nd Most spots: 2nd; C. Biggest: 2nd. Longest hair: 1st Most spots: 3rd

47. Rhyming stones:
more, four, sore, door, bore, roar

48. Jigwords:

B	E	E	T	L	E
S	P	I	D	E	R
E	A	R	W	I	G
L	O	C	U	S	T
W	E	E	V	I	L
H	O	R	N	E	T

49. Word count: donkey

50. Tricky T-shirts:

51. Snakes and ladders:
Cate finished

52. 3-D shapes:

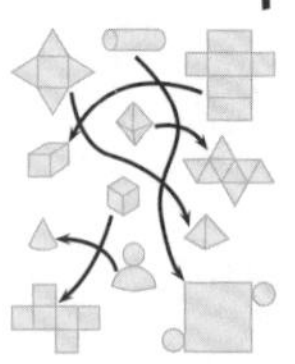

53. Secret code: You will find instructions for your mission in the hollow tree.

54. Pasta pieces: 69

55. Coconut palm:

56. Pirate Pete:

57. Picture crossword:

r	a	d	i	o
o		u		g
b	a	k	e	r
i		e		e
n	o	s	e	s

58. Cross country: Canada

59. Opposite pairs: clear

60. Cross-sum:

	18↓	12↓	24↓	
12→	8	1	3	13↓
20→	4	5	9	2
18→	6	2	7	3
	17→	4	5	8

61. Mini-sudoku:

4	1	3	2
2	3	1	4
3	4	2	1
1	2	4	3

62. Back to the start: 3

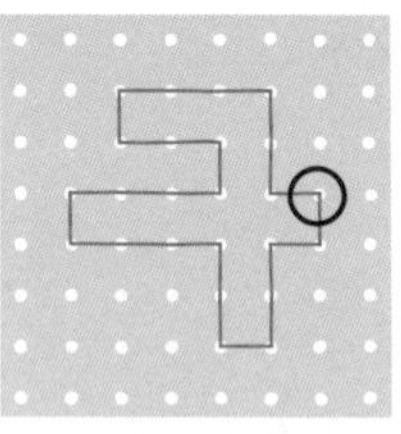

63. Spider's web: tarantula

64. Fairytale mix-up:
1. Goldilocks 2. Little Red Riding Hood 3. Snow White 4. Hansel and Gretel 5. Cinderella 6. Sleeping Beauty

65. Missing shapes:
1. A 2. C

66. Secret code: Meet me at the railway station at six pm on Thursday. I will carry red roses.

67. Have a heart: 1. in**fan**ts 2. f**arm**er 3. c**row**ds 4. s**tar**tle 5. st**one**s 6. c**run**ch 7. w**ash**es

68. Pirate Pete's treasure:

69. Crazy talk: 1. Hello! My name is Sam and I am eight. 2. Please can you tell me the way to the station? 3. Please may I go to the park to play with Ashley? 4. Where did you buy your shoes? They're really cool.

70. Alphablocks:

71. Pizza pieces: C

72. How many penguins: B

73. Crossword:

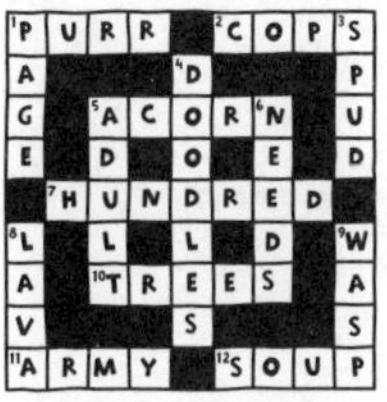

74. Find the beetle:

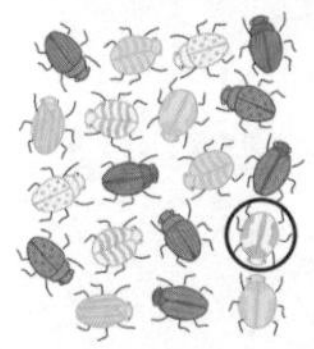

75. Whose pet?:
Salim: parrot Ruby: dog
Kayla: hamster Noah: fish

76. Spot the starfish:

77. Lost jewels:
1. pearl 2. diamond 3. ruby
4. emerald 5. sapphire

78. Farmyard jumble: 8

79. On the bus:

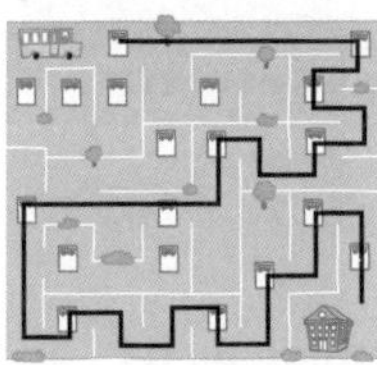

80. Word cross:
1. T 2. G 3. Y 4. M

81. Number monster:
1. 13+24=37 2. 9+3=12
3. 8+6=14

82. Shapes and boxes:

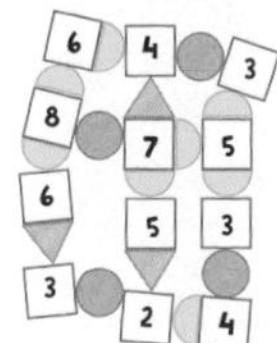

83. Lively letters: 1. calm
2. stop 3. pears 4. dread
5. thin 6. never 7. finger

84. Riddle grid: your name

85. Camouflage:

86. What's the link?:
1. jack 2. horse 3. work 4. frog
5. cross 6. corn 7. house

87. Odd ones out: 1. rocket
2. bucket 3. ruler 4. hotel
5. chicken

89. Campsite jigsaw: B, D

90. Dotty dominoes:

1. 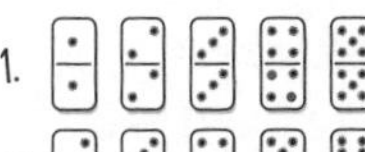

2. 

3. 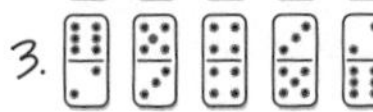

4.

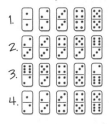

91. Shredded words:

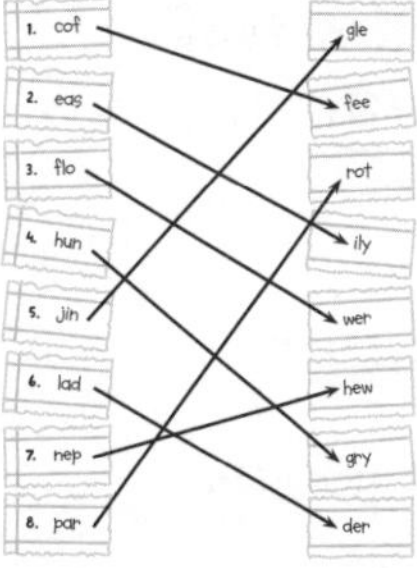

92. Boat race: Bluebird: 4th
Rose: 1st Skylark: 2nd Tulip: 3rd

93. Word count: tongue

94. Hopping frog: flower: 4
dragonfly: 10 snail: 14 duckling: 18

95. Zoo crisscross:

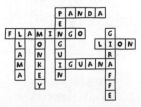

97. Cross-sum:

		11↓	9↓
	12↓ 10→	4	8
6→	3	2	1
12→	7	5	

98. Jumbled jokes:

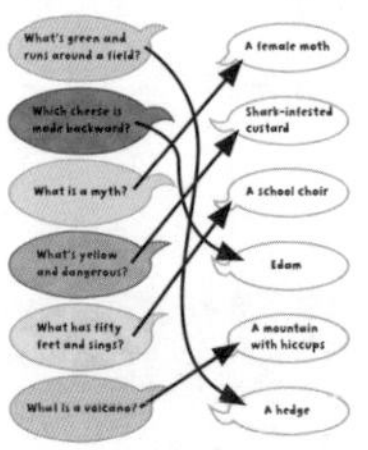

99. Identical fins:

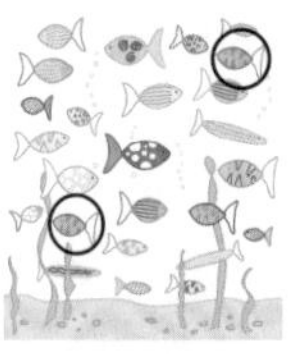

100. Find the city:
San Francisco

101. Name game: Joseph

102. Giant beanstalk:
3(+4): ...15.23..35..47
6(+4): ..14....34, 38..

103. Arctic animals:

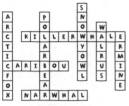

ARCTICFOX
POLARBEAR
SNOWYOWL
WALRUS
KILLERWHALE
ERMINE
CARIBOU
NARWHAL

104. On target: Rufus: 11
Eva: 7 Chris: 11 **Violet: 12**

105. Ferris wheel: 11

106. Spelling secrets:
expect a man in black
do not fear he is a friend

107. Odd gnome out: F

108. Doorsteps:

35
19 16
10 9 7
5 5 4 3
3 2 3 1 2

109. Nursery rhyme mix-up:
1. Humpty Dumpty
2. Old MacDonald
3. Little Jack Horner
4. Three blind mice
5. Jack and Jill
6. The Grand old Duke of York

110. Desert crisscross:

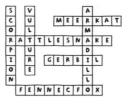

SCORPION
VULTURE
ARMADILLO
MEERKAT
RATTLESNAKE
GERBIL
FENNECFOX

111. Robot power:

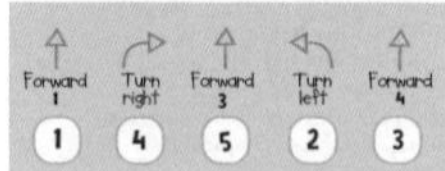

112. Thumbprint maze:

113. Island in the sun:
Barbados

114. Capital quiz
Paris: France
London: United Kingdom
Washington, DC: United States
Beijing: China
Canberra: Australia
Tokyo: Japan
Moscow: Russia

115. Beach pairs:

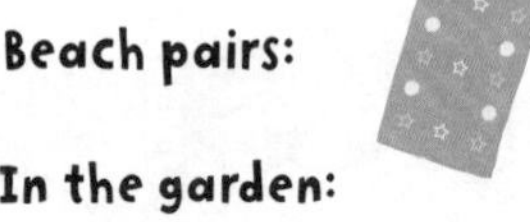

117. In the garden:

118. Cross-sum:

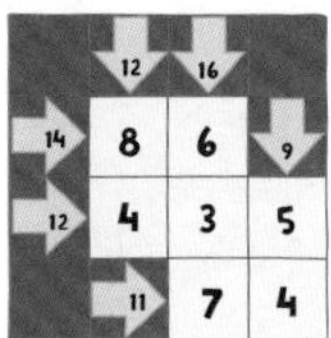

119. Number monster:
1. 14−7=7 2. 22−14=8
3. 15−6=9

120. Number cross:

1.

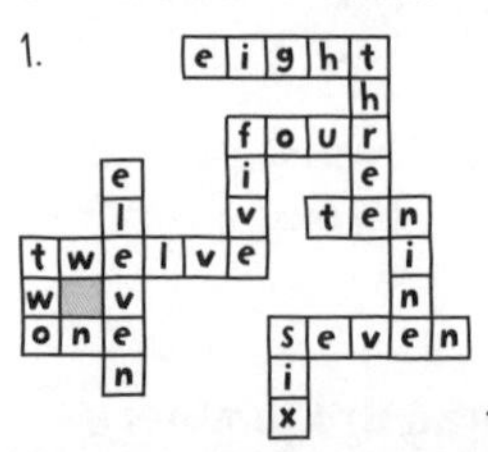

2. four

121. What am I?:
1. door 2. less

122. Optical illusions:
1. no 2. straight

123. Perfect pies:
Cheese and leek pie: 8:05
Vegetable pie: 7:55 Fish pie: 7:50
Chicken and mushroom pie: 7:40

124. Dotty dominoes:

125. Buried treasure:
1. 4,1 2,3 3,4 2. 4,3

126. Crossword:

1 p	a	r	t		2 w	o	l	3 f
o				4 c				i
d		5 a	w	a	r	6 d		r
s		s		m		i		e
	7 c	h	e	e	t	a	h	
8 t		e		l		r		9 g
i		10 s	t	o	r	y		i
n				t				r
11 y	e	a	r		12 h	o	w	l

127. Weighing in: 10, 30

128. Funny faces:

129. Mirror message:
Things don't seem so everyday when you look at them in a different way.

130. Sounds the same:
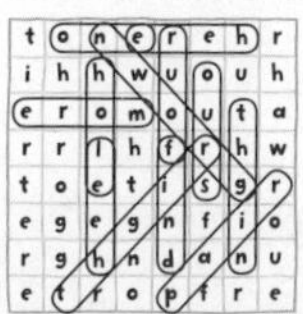

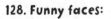

131. Train parts: B

132. Beach treasure hunt: 1

133. Shell search:
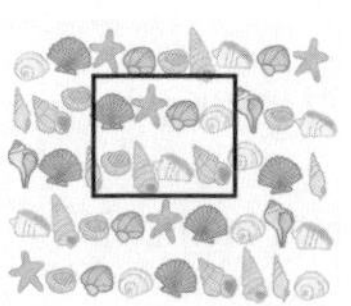

135. Umbrella patterns: 2

136. Sneaky letters:

W	I	S	H	L	A	M	B	S	T	O	O	L
T	O	P	C	O	U	L	D	B	R	E	W	S
N	I	C	E	A	N	S	W	E	R	S	U	N
F	L	O	W	E	R	H	O	N	E	S	T	Y
I	T	C	R	U	M	B	R	I	V	E	R	S
B	R	A	V	E	K	N	I	G	H	T	M	E
N	O	S	E	W	R	I	T	E	C	A	R	D
T	U	B	E	G	N	O	M	E	A	R	M	Y
O	F	M	U	S	C	L	E	T	H	I	N	K

137. Same meaning:
1. ✓ 2. ✗ 3. ✓ 4. ✓ 5. ✗ 6. ✓ 7. ✗ 8. ✗

138. Cupcake numbers:
1. 1, 5, 7, 11 2. Yes: cupcake 12

139. Calendar crisscross:
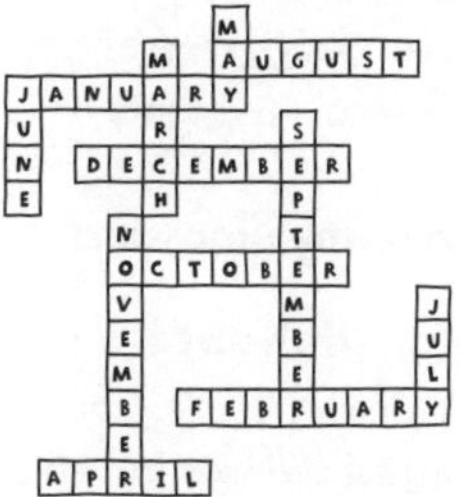

140. Alphablocks:

141. Windsurfing:

142. Missing symbol:

143. Picture parts:
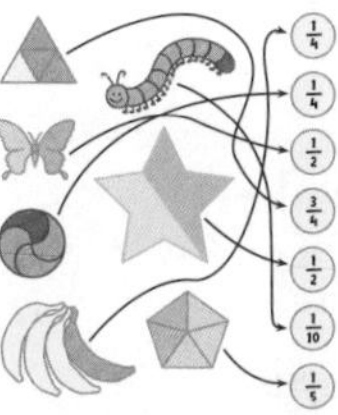

144. Microphone mix-up:
Green microphone

145. X-words:
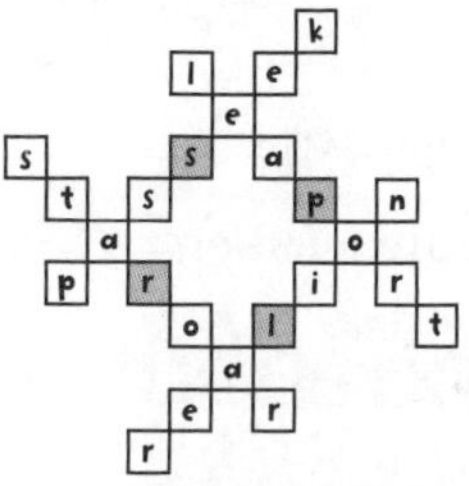

146. Advanced archery:
William: 22 Robin: 22
Howard: 25 Artemis: 24

147. Souvenir shuffle:
Amber: fan from Japan
Jake: cap from Canada Louis: Ukelele from Hawaii Mei: Toy windmill from the Netherlands

148. Alphablocks:

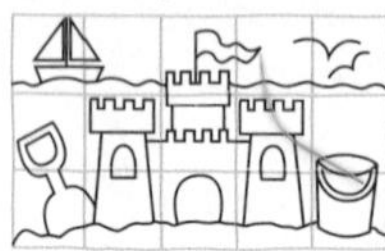

149. Word ladder: bags, rags, rage, race, pace, pack

150. What goes where?:

151. Crossnumber:

	6			1	3	
1	0	1			6	6
6		0		4	5	
	1	4		1		2
1	2			1	1	1
	3	6			5	

152. Whose fish?: Yellow fish: Jimbo Purple fish: Rocky Green fish: Andy Orange fish: Johnny

153. House numbers:

154. X-words:

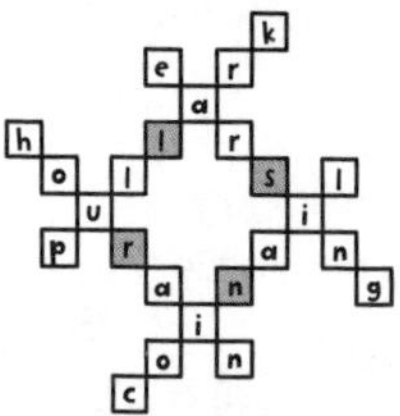

155. Ocean cube: A, E

157. Odd ones out: 1. lemon 2. mouth 3. spider 4. size 5. penguin

158. Toothpaste tangle: C

159. What goes where?:

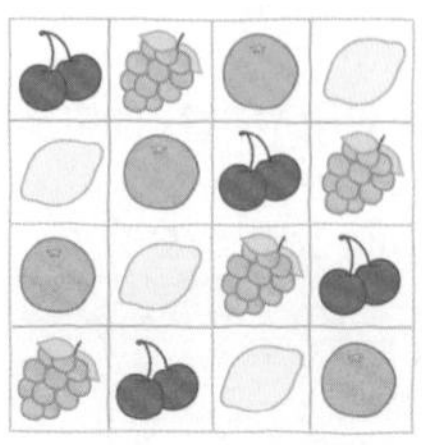

161. Where am I going?:
James: Disneyland Paris
Maya: Yellowstone National Park
Taleisha: Legoland Copenhagen

162. Where do they eat...?:
Pizza: Italy
Fish and chips: England
Chow mein: China
Hamburger: USA
Haggis: Scotland
Curry: India Sushi: Japan
Nachos: Mexico Snails: France

163. How many dinosaurs: 8

164. Polar alphabet: Welcome to the North Pole. I am away fishing but feel free to shelter in my igloo. Best wishes from Koolik

165. It's all Greek to me Phidias the artist made this vase – do not drop it!

166. Calculate this!: 42

167. Odd crab out:

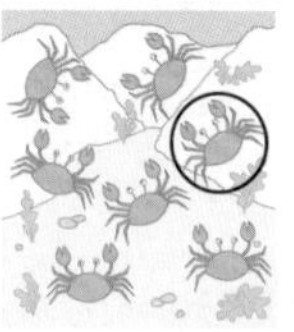

169. Ship shapes:

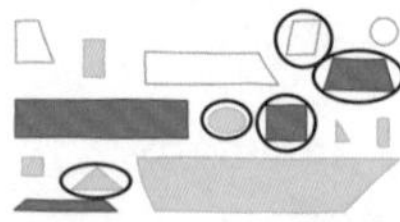

170. Animal cube: B

171. Word ladder: surf, sure, cure, care, cave, wave

172. Planet puzzle: 1. Mercury 2. Mars 3. **V**enus 4. **E**arth 5. **N**eptune 6. **U**ranus 7. **S**aturn 8. Jupiter (**VENUS**)

173. Busy bees:

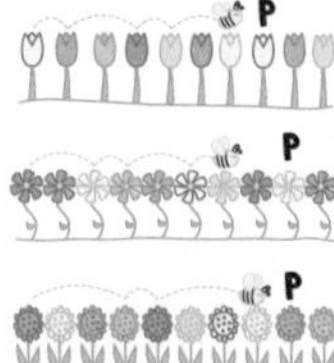

174. Counting squares: 11

175. Bus trip: Blue: 30 Red: 20 Green: 50

176. Magical creatures: